STARDUST

STEALING THE SUN: BOOK 8

RON COLLINS

SKYFOX
PUBLISHING
Science Fiction

STARDUST

STEALING THE SUN: BOOK 8

Cover Design: © Ron Collins
All rights reserved

Cover Image
© Ig0rzh | Dreamstime.com

Skyfox Publishing

ISBN-10: 1-946176-38-9
ISBN-13: 978-1-946176-38-7

STEALING THE SUN

includes

STARFLIGHT

STARBURST

STARFALL

STARCLASH

STARBOUND

STARCRASH

STARGAMES

STARDUST

STARBORN

Other Work by Ron Collins

Wakers

The Knight Deception
A Trevin Knight Thriller

Saga of the God-Touched Mage

Glamour of the God-Touched
Target of the Orders
Trail of the Torean
Gathering of the God-Touched
Pawn of the Planewalker
Changing of the Guard
Lord of the Freeborn
Lords of Existence

Picasso's Cat & Other Stories

Five Magics

Seven Days in May

Tomorrow in All the Worlds

Follow Ron at:
http://www.typosphere.com
Twitter: @roncollins13

This one is for my dad

To live is to suffer, to survive is to find some meaning in the suffering.

Friedrich Nietzsche

CONTENTS

INTRODUCTION

I am of a generation who, when I hear the term *stardust*, I think of Joni Mitchell and of Woodstock. It's hard for me to hear that word and not think of that song.

Yeah. I think that means I might be either old, or getting into that area of old.

Don't break my bubble there, okay?

Regardless, one of the things that I knew I was biting off when I started writing this book was the effort of working across time—and space, of course! When we first find Torrance Black at the *Everguard* Systems Command desk way back in book 1, he's a young guy. Time waits for no one, though. I admit that's something that's been on my mind as I wrote this one.

It's a pretty dark book in places.

We are, after all, going back to Esgarat (he says letting that quadar out of the bag), and as we recall from book 6, there's a lot of, ahem, shit going down there. Torrance is starlocked, so to speak, and the Families have begun to flex their real muscles. And, of course, there's this little problem with their primary star Alpha Centauri A—hence the cause of their dust, right?

Time is passing for them.

The clock is ticking.

Something's got to give.

Given things going on in both our external world (pandemics, and wars, and capitalistic elements running more than a little bit amok), and inside the little sphere of my family (health things and elderly parent things), it's been both a difficult and enlightening book to write. I often say I come to the page to learn what I really think about certain things, and this book has helped me do some of that thinking.

With luck it'll be an equally interesting one to read—but I don't really get a say on that, now, do I?

Anyway, it's been fun to work with the weird timelines that *Stealing the Sun* works over, and fun to work in a world where both relativistic and multidimensional FTL issues need to be dealt with. It's been fun to write aging characters and fun to write new generations coming along behind them.

I really, really love these characters. All of them, really.

I hope you do too.

Ron Collins
2022

PROLOGUE

Esgarat City
Local Season: Eldoro Leading, Year of Second *Piela*, Cycle 57

Esgarat City's streets radiated the tension Baraq Waganat expected they would. Something was happening. The world was ready to crack, ready to crumble under the weight of its Families.

He felt it as he moved down the central street.

Anxious, peering from under the lip of his hood, he glanced at the sky.

Both the greater heat of Eldoro and the lesser of Katon had already slipped below the horizon, but the edge of the dome above retained an orange glow that felt warm against the clouded sky. The air in the streets was growing crisp, though. The shadows darker.

Baraq understood things better now.

He understood this struggle was bigger than simply retaliating against his own Family and his own brother—now the leader of that Family. Tierra had killed Baraq's son for rebelling against Family control, and for actively arguing against the Council of Clans. Baraq could still picture the scene, Tierra leading the rest of the Families on their killing spree, murdering Brada, and butchering hundreds of the *hedgie* riffraff with him.

At first Baraq had focused his fight against only his brother, against only his own Waganat Family. They had been the problem, as he saw it.

But the mountain raid had shown him the full nature of the truth.

Tierra Waganat was simply the head of the lizard.

The Families had joined in Tierra's retaliation.

They had followed Baraq as he'd traveled to Louratna's outpost, and they had brazenly attacked her independent quadars.

Having left the compound earlier, he remembered watching that action from afar, too. Watched as the Families destroyed the facility and slaughtered Louratna's workers. Watched as they had marched Louratna out into the open, then executed her like she was a common criminal.

He pushed his clenched fists deeper into his robe's internal pockets.

Yes, Baraq thought as his gaze skimmed the orange sky.

The rot inside the Families went deeper than he'd understood.

I will have my revenge.

That thought had consumed him throughout his return trek from Louratna's compound. It had eaten at his insides as he scrambled through the rough mountains, and it had consumed him as he ate wild roots and drank from morning *katja* plants each early heat, all while crawling his way back to the city.

He worried for the lower families and independent *hedgie* quadars, but there was nothing to do for them.

What Brada said in his speeches was true.

The Families would not stop unless someone stopped them. Tierra's action against lower *hedgie* families set the stage. When the Families destroyed Louratna's outpost, they removed the only remaining force outside Esgarat City that could have opposed them. Without the need to pretend otherwise, the strongest Families would sort through the remnants of the *hedgie* population, and fight to further consolidate power.

That was going to be bloody.

Baraq could not save the *hedgies* from bloodshed. He was only one quadar, and a poor one at that.

The thoughts were bitter.

In trying to save his world he'd ruined everything he'd ever touched. Even Crissandr. Especially Crissandr, his beautiful and wise *kalla* who he had turned away.

He had lived his whole life under the idea that Family leadership was necessary. That it was only natural that the Families controlled everything. Families understood the world. The Families knew what needed to be done. Family leadership made All of Esgarat better.

That failure would burn in Baraq's stomachs until the day the mountain reclaimed him.

At least he had left the Waganat compound in rubble in return for that misguidance.

It was a start, anyway.

He would have that revenge.

And if—in the process of enacting that revenge—Baraq Waganat could damage the Families and thereby help the *hedgies*, that would do. From this point forward, as long as he was alive, he would do his best to walk in his son's shoes, but it would be a trip taken with the point of a dagger, or—the thought made him grimly grin—the point of a gun.

Nothing else was left for him but that bitter declaration.

Still, his heart could not help but take in the glorious dome of the sky lit above him tonight.

It was a good sign, he thought.

The forces of nature were on his side.

When he was a young quadar this time of the heat had been the moment he liked best—the time when the dryness of the day radiated from the city's stonework to clash with the cooler air that came with darkness. When he was younger, of course, that glow came as a gauzy coloring from behind the clouds, and the clash was not so bold. Now the sky's coloring felt sharp and edgy, like a smooth crystal bowl looming over the city, waiting to shatter and rain its crystalline shards down over the ground.

Now, the drop from heat to chill made his joints ache. Perhaps it was just because he was getting older, perhaps not.

The world was changing so fast.

FUNERAL

CHAPTER 1

Esgarat Mountains
Local Season: Eldoro Leading, Year of Second *Piela*, Cycle 57

The Families' attack had been as brutal as it was swift.

Those still living collected the dead—the *indati*, as quadarti knew them—stacking their bodies into rotting piles that lined the caves and caverns where those free quadars had once lived. The toll in numbers was immense. The toll in what it meant to the science those dead quadars had been working on was impossible to determine.

Louratna, their leader and the driver of the entire mountain society, had been executed—shot by a Tegra gun placed behind her head, and left facedown to bleed her life liquid onto the dusty stone floor of her mountain compound.

The rocket program was shattered, the laboratories, factories, and testing rigs destroyed.

The Families from All of Esgarat did not understand the ramifications of that last damage—could not understand the fate this destruction doomed the quadarti to. They did not see the truth of the land's imminent death, so even if those Families had been told the purpose of these factories was to save all of life as this planet knew it, they would not have believed it. If they had understood their doom, there would have been no attack at all. No dead quadars. No wreckage under the mountains.

Instead, all that the Families knew was that Baraq Waganat—the traitor who had desecrated his own Family name—had come to this nook of the mountain, and that he had met with Louratna and her group of ideological heretics.

They knew Baraq was a renegade aligned with Lelo, the first member of the Waganat Family who had gone bad.

Yes, they knew that much.

Baraq Waganat was a traitor.

And, since he was meeting with Louratna in her secretive caverns, then she, too, was a traitor.

The Families, led by the Waganats themselves, had simply done what they always did.

After their damage had been enacted, the Families left behind the remaining quadars—and the lone human being—to first recover these limp bodies and then to patch together what they would do next.

An argument ensued.

The fundamentalists and traditionalists among the survivors wanted to return each of the dead quadars to the mountain from which they had come. Wanted to carry them downward through the caverns and the cracks, one by one, down through the shafts and breaks that ages of water flowing through the depths of those passages had carved into the ancient basalt of their homeland. "We are all made of mountain," they said. "We should take them to the dark waters that still run deep. We should leave them for Esgarat to take back as they will."

That was true quadarti way, they said.

It was the way of the elders.

Those of more modern temperaments disagreed.

The bodies should be covered and scented properly, then taken to be laid in the desert.

"The quadarti rose from the mountain long ago," the argument went. "Better to give them to the harsh lands that have been our home for many times longer than any one of them were able to remember." All of Esgarat now included the desert lands and the creatures that roamed them, they said. If the quadarti were meant to stay under the mountain, they would never have crawled upward to begin with.

In the end, the modern faction was victorious.

They would take the horrifyingly large mound of dead quadars to the dry, barren lands and leave them for the desert to take them in.

The victory, however, had little to do with ideology or theology and everything to do with basic mathematics.

There were simply too many bodies.

Given the number of dead the ride to the desert would be hard but given the number of those remaining, carrying so many dead to the depths of the mountain would be impossible.

CHAPTER 2

As tradition mandated, the quadarti waited to perform the rite until late in the heat when Eldoro was nearly set—when the transition from light to darkness would aid the dead in finding their way home. That time was coming shortly. Which meant there was work to do. Even though—out here in the vast stretches of the cloudless desert where there was nothing to shield the radiation—heat from that nearly set Eldoro combined with the lesser heat of Katon to forge an omnipresent hammer that beat down like fire.

For the third time, Torrance Black stood at one side of the cart and slid a body forward, clutching the harsh fabrics at the shoulder and waist of the fallen quadar then striding as strongly as he could to carry its mass to its final place in the sand.

His vision swooned.

The gauzy robe he wore billowed in the blast-furnace of a hard wind that whipped a raggedy rhythm around his shoulders and burned sand across his exposed cheekbones.

His thighs ached with effort as his feet slipped over the sand.

His knees throbbed, and the muscles of his arms and lower back burned with pain as hot as the winds. The dead quadar was so heavy it slipped from one hand, and Torrance had to go to a knee to prevent the indignity of losing the quadar inside. Gasping for air, he took in so much dust and grit that his lungs seized.

Excited quadars chattered in the misty distance, but all Torrance could do was to focus on breathing.

He gave a huge cough. His throat burned.

"Come up, Torranze," Crissandr said into his ear as he finally came to realize he wasn't going to die on the spot. "Come up," she said again, kneeling beside him and helping him to his feet. "Take refuge."

She guided him to the empty flatbed cart that until a moment ago had been full with quadar dead. Cupping her large hand over his skull, she pressed him downward toward a shaded spot under the cart.

Embarrassed, but also feeling the steel brace of survival instinct clamping down, Torrance let her direct him to slide into a slanted slice of shade under the flatbed. Panting hard, he pulled folds of cloth from over his head and let them lay loose across the back of his neck.

For an instant, the gusting breeze almost felt cool.

The slats of the flatbed cart above him let a few harsh lines of Eldoro's sharpness fall over his face. At least they'd finished that load.

There were more carts, though.

More bodies. More lines.

He was embarrassed. Sitting here and watching while others did the work he couldn't manage. He had joined in for as long as he could, though it had been only three times he'd carried bodies. Only three. He put his head in his hands, trying to pretend he was not the most useless creature in all the planets.

This was the bottom, he thought.

Burying Louratna and the rest of her quadars.

This was the worst it could get.

Torrance had lived most of his life with the understanding that he had no great power, that he was just a guy—an LC rather than Commander, a simple systems grunt rather than a role that required any true leadership. Even his role as Science Ambassador had been more window dressing than not.

He had begun to think differently here, though.

Since he'd been shipwrecked on Eden, Torrance had worked with these quadars to develop an entire rocket program out of thin air. A program that could have lifted them up. That in the right moment might have saved the entire species. He had begun to feel like, just maybe, he might be worth something—that he might be exceptional in some way, that he might be a great man in all the ways that it meant to be genuinely great.

Now here he was.

That entire project was dead, and he was cowering under the half-assed shade of a flatbed cart while someone else did work he couldn't manage.

He lifted his head from his hands.

The few strands of hair he had left fluttered in the wind. His senses grew clogged with the grit of rock and dust. He was sweating hard despite wearing the light robe. Quadar physiology may have evolved to deal with the twin heats of Eldoro and Katon, but he was a human being. His body was not configured to handle this world.

He was getting older, too.

Older and more fragile.

He wondered how much longer he could last on this planet where he'd guess the temperatures were now rising to the 50s Celsius in midday before crashing to something as unbearably cold in the evenings.

He remembered the science reports he'd once consumed about the planet humans called Eden, but that the quadars called Esgarat. Heat profiles. Climate estimations. Mineral composition. At one point Torrance Black thought he might be the galaxy's leading intellectual when it came to Eden.

And yet, how little he knew.

He swallowed a dry breath.

Giving up any aspirations that he was ever going to be able to truly contribute, Torrance watched the quadars do their grisly work, lifting each fabric-wrapped body from its cart to lay them in straight columns that stretched ahead of him.

Torrance watched them speak with each other.

Watched them exchange ideas as they worked together to leverage weight. Watched their expressions harden with each new delivery of a friend or a clutch-mate to the lanes of dead they created. Their shoulders sagged in the heat of their work. Their centrals closed tight against the heat and the sand. The pores of their skin opened across wide back plates, giving their bodies maximum surface air for cooling. Their primaries burned with amber flares in the slanted crisscross of light from the dual heats of Eldoro and Katon—Alpha Centauri A and Alpha Centauri B—whose orbital position were now such that the quadars' shadows made diamondlike patterns of shadow on the hard plate ground around them.

He took in glances made between them through the slits and flaps of the filmy turbanlike scarves they wrapped around themselves in such intricate fashions as to leave both their primaries and centrals exposed while covering all else.

Their expressions contained grief, and loss, and dismay.

They were at once so alien to everything he'd grown up with, yet so much like the human being he was.

Torrance crossed his legs before him, then rubbed his thighs and his cramping calves.

We are all stardust, he thought, recalling a poem from back home. It had seemed trite at the time, but now he watched these creatures work and he wondered.

How much different were the quadars from humans he had known?

Their bodies diverged, of course —with their six fingers to a hand, and the multihued grayed tints of their skin. They had three hearts, three stomachs, and three eyes. Their lips were spare.

He could go on. Perhaps he should.

The idea of himself listing the physiology of the quadars like some distant anthropologist came over him.

It was a silly idea, though.

He discounted it as soon as he thought it.

Still, the image of him doing that made him shift his frame.

Louratna and Marisa Harthing.

His throat constricted as the unbidden comparison came to him. In very real but vastly different ways, those were the two loves of his life. Both women were equally pragmatic as they were idealistic. Both were brilliant. Both driven.

Both enjoyed food.

Both had intricate senses of humor.

Both had taught him things about himself that he hadn't seen before they arrived in his life.

They had each given Torrance everything he needed.

In the end, how different were they?

Quadar bodies had evolved so differently in their environments, but how much different were Marisa and Louratna in things that really mattered?

"Torranze!"

Crissandr, the quadarti mate of Baraq Waganat and one-time friend of Louratna, stood at a distance, at the midpoint of the middle line of quadarti dead, her central eye closed and the back of her hand shading her primaries from under her wrap.

"It is time."

He nodded.

The carts were empty, the bodies, wrapped in mourning, lay in those three long rows that stretched across the hard-packed desert like a road to the horizon.

He sipped from a water skin, then set it aside, letting his fingertips rest there for the briefest of moments. Something about the feel of those skins calmed him. Its leather was soft against his hands, made from the hide of a *tal* beast no different from those the quadars had used to drive the cartloads of bodies far enough out to the desert to perform this rite.

Torrance pulled bands of fabric back up to protect his neck and back, then ducked his head and rolled over the hard-packed sand to stand upright.

He stepped past each fabric-draped mound, unable to keep from flashing on the string of funerals he'd attended after the *Everguard* disaster.

Flags draped over coffins.

Cards placed against urns.

The fabrics here were more pragmatic than the United Government's had been. They were harsh burlap of a sort woven from fibers made with *katja* root, dark tan, a color that from a distance would disappear into his heat-warped vision of the cracked desert landscape.

He sensed their differences deeply now, thinking about Louratna.

Flags draping the coffins that had held *Everguard*'s dead were made to be honorifics to the service of those dead—as well as vivid reminders to the living as symbols of why they should continue to fight.

These fabrics, however, were used simply to keep sand from the dead as they were preparing for their last trips. They would degrade rapidly and provide ease of access for the desert itself.

Crissandr stood next to Louratna's body.

Arriving at her side, Torrance stood still, feeling the beat of the wind ripple over the contours of his hood, sensing its pressure against his back, trying hard not to cry but unable to tear his gaze away from the fabric around Louratna's head and shoulders.

He thought of his time spent with her.

Remembered working together to create a hybrid language, which they called qualish, that could roll off both their tongues.

Remembered sharing food.

Remembered teaching each other.

Over the wind and through the heat, her voice came to him then. No words. Just the tone, and her simple inflection.

The weight of Crissandr's head pressed against his shoulder in the same way Louratna sometimes did when they had stayed up latc discussing physics. He waited until Crissandr pulled it away, then knelt to put his hand on Louratna's arm.

As wind blew sand across her, he recalled when he had told Louratna about the wormhole pod that *Everguard* launched that had started this whole mess, recalled how his skin had seemed to sizzle when she revealed parts of the pod's torn remains to him.

He recalled, too, watching the moment of her death. Saw her thrown to her knees, a Family warrior behind her with a gun.

The crack of the weapon.

Her body lying dead on the ground.

The bitter need for vengeance surged through him then.

Torrance had felt that need in every moment since, but it was only then, feeling the bony remains of Louratna's body—the curve of her shoulder that would lead to the nape of her neck—that he understood how wrong that need was. How limited that most human of emotions would be.

His throat constricted with an infinite sense of loss.

"I was wrong," he said, recalling words he'd had with Edart Kel, the youthful engineer who had helped design the rockets that now flew.

How do we rebuild? Edart had asked after the Families had destroyed Louratna's rocket program.

We don't, he had replied in stunned shock.

But that had been wrong.

Kneeling beside Louratna's body, Torrance knew better.

He closed his hand over Louratna's fabric-covered shoulder.

"I was wrong," he said to her again. "We will build it back. You can trust me on this."

The rockets would fly again. That much was certain.

When Torrance rose, he saw Crissandr was weeping.

He opened his arms and they embraced.

Even in the desert heat, she was warm against his chest.

He held her tight for several moments, feeling her tremble and giving her time. His own eyes watered up as he scanned the rows of dead. Already mounds of sand were building over the windward side of the bodies.

The desert would not need long to take them back.

CHAPTER 3

The sky above was a cloudless dome of blue as the quadars' funeral excursion made its way back across the hard desert, back toward their mountain home.

Torrance sat in the back of the cart, rolling with its sway, baking despite the burlap sheets spread over top of the cart to block the heat's rays. Wheels creaked on axles. *Tal* beast hooves clomped on desert ground. He had long since lost his ability to smell the beasts, though their odor was strong.

The desert was simply the desert, now.

Crissandr sat silently beside him.

Four others had taken positions on the other side of the platform. They chatted quietly.

The blue of the sky was a different hue from Earth's, Torrance thought. Close enough, though. Close enough that he could easily forget the difference.

If he didn't know better, if he were simply a wandering space pilot who stumbled upon this place today, he would have assumed the sky had always been as it was now—open desert under an expansive and cloudless sky. But Torrance *did* know better. It was his hand and his programming that had sent the wormhole pod here to begin with—the Taranth Stone, as it was known on Eden, or the Light That Fell from the Sky.

All the science Torrance had seen said the clouds that cloaked the planet were permanent fixtures, which, in what he now saw with a horrible sense of irony, was among the things certain politicians used to justify the stance of ignoring the planet as they voted against sending explorations here.

He'd heard quadarti histories now, too.

How, until a spare handful of cycles before, the skies had always been covered with clouds, how the heats of Eldoro and Katon—Alpha Centauri A and B—had been blurs in the gauzy multihued overcast that was always there. How only when those clouds had been burned away had tiny Eterdane—as the quadarti named Proxima—been revealed.

"What are you to do?" Crissandr asked him.

The cart jostled as a wheel caught a rut.

Torrance grabbed a rail by his seat and waited while Crissandr rearranged herself. Ahead, the *tal* beast pulling the cart snorted and plodded away.

Communicating with Crissandr was more difficult than with Louratna, or Edart for that matter, because, though he had been around Crissandr often, the two had communicated less intensely than he had with either of the others. The form of qualish they shared wasn't as robust. The tone to her question, though, combined with the distant aura of her gaze, still focused on open desert, made him take an extra moment to form his thoughts so that Crissandr would understand.

There was another reason for his delay, though.

One he realized more fully as he took in her pensive profile.

He did not want to hurt her, yet there was a good chance he might have to.

"You are worried," he finally said. He had wanted to say *afraid* but realized the only word they had together was something more like *worried*, so he'd used that instead.

"Not worried," she replied. "*Scaza.*"

"*Scaza,*" he said, letting his tongue play with the word. "*Scaza,*" he said again, committing it to memory. He hoped it meant *afraid* but wouldn't know for sure unless he tried it in different moments.

Her attention was on him now, though.

Crissandr had turned her gaze to his, and he felt its weight as certainly as he felt each roll and each jolt of the platform below him.

"First," he said, "we must get back to where we were."

"Then?"

"Well," Torrance said. He sighed, trying to decide how deeply to answer the question.

The first idea he and Louratna had focused on was to build a single big rocket that could send quadars back toward Earth, but they both realized the farcical nature of that idea as soon as they did some simple projections. The planet—at least as it was today—was simply incapable of supporting that kind of sophistication.

Louratna proposed a rocket sent into Eldoro—Alpha Centauri A—to break its bonds to the spaceships that were draining the star, but Torrance explained he had no idea how to do that.

They had fallen back on a different plan.

"The idea was to send rockets into the upper..." He paused there.

Only he and Louratna had a shared understanding of the idea of *atmosphere*, hence a shared term for it. Torrance struggled to find a replacement that would work.

"Into the highest sky," he said.

"Make clouds."

He gave a click that tried to mimic the quadars' quick tone for an affirmative. "Yes. Make clouds."

"And clouds will save us?"

He hoped he kept his expression stoic enough, or that Crissandr wasn't adroit enough to pick up on human expressions—though he didn't believe that was a good bet. Crissandr's strength had always been her empathy.

He looked at her, not wanting to lie.

The goal had been to keep the planet from burning up during what he saw as a second phase of the changes that were coming Eden's way. But it had always been a stopgap. The draining of Eldoro would not stop, and eventually it would lead to disaster regardless of what happened now. The first phase of change had been the burning of Eden's natural sulfurous cloud cover. It had happened more quickly than Torrance had expected. His arms and hands had scars from times he'd been caught out in its acidic rains.

This second stage could be worse.

Temperatures were already rocketing upward as, without the reflective cover of its clouds, Eden's atmosphere now let raw heat through, then captured it again in a greenhouse lensing affect. Torrance was no climate expert, so he had no frame of reference to determine how long this stage could last, but he could see it was already affecting the planet's fundamental processes. Plants were stunting, then dying. Predators were overhunting prey that he'd guess were now finding ever-shrinking zones of habitable land.

So, seeding cloud cover was mostly there to buy time.

Slow down the change and keep the planet from burning up in a geological blink of an eye.

It could still work—but in the end that would only get them so far. In fact, this act of saving the planet in the short term could well hasten the decline of life here once the energy from Alpha Centauri A fell too low.

There had to be something else.

Thinking about that something else made him acutely aware of Crissandr's presence. He could not lie to her.

"No," he said. "Clouds will not save All of Esgarat forever."

She nodded, mimicking his human motion, then put her head in her hands.

"I need to find Baraq," he said, knowing that the mention of her pair-mate would draw pain.

Baraq Waganat was the only quadar Torrance knew who understood the full depths of what they were working on. Baraq would never be a replacement for Louratna, but the fact that he had come to Louratna in search of rocketry he could use to sway a fight his way meant he saw certain possibilities. Louratna and Torrance had turned him away, though. Their work was too important.

Afterward, though, Louratna had described Baraq's full story.

Now Torrance felt like he understood Baraq better, and with Louratna gone, he thought hard about the quadar. Could he work with Baraq Waganat?

Baraq needed rockets.

Torrance needed workers—a lot of workers.

If ever there was a situation where a deal seemed logical, this was it.

He could use a collaborator, too. That was always how he worked best. Louratna had described Baraq as an inventor at heart.

Could he help?

So, Torrance was going to find Baraq.

And he was going to offer that deal.

Torrance would give Baraq the rockets he needed to win a war.

In return he would ask Baraq to focus workers on making a rocket big enough to make it to deep space.

He would send a new message.

This time a physical one, one that the Solar System could neither miss nor ignore.

He looked at Crissandr, hoping his actions wouldn't hurt her.

Her expression was difficult to read.

There was pain in it, yes. There was loss. And anger. But there was more there. More in the way her shoulders rose with her breathing and her fingers drew the edge of her *haldi* up to her neckline. Her primaries slitted against a sudden gust of wind, and the line of her lips flattened with an essence that made Torrance deeply aware of her presence.

Resolve.

That's what her expression was.

Resolve, and something else that, though he had no word for the emotion Crissandr's bearing carried in that moment, Torrance felt it so deeply he knew it for a universal truth.

She pressed her hand onto his knee then, each of her six fingers seeming to etch themselves into the meat of his body.

"I need to find Baraq, too," she said. "We will go together."

BEGINNINGS

CHAPTER 4

The rains had come to the city earlier in the heat, their thunder rattling its buildings and towers, their torrents dousing its streets and sending denizens scampering for cover.

The *tal* beast's hooves echoed in the quiet aftermath as it pulled the Waganat carriage between the cavernlike walls of shops and tall buildings that lined the way to the Tegra compound. Through the cabin's open windows, the currents made by their motion brought in air that felt cleansed and smelled almost sweet.

A few shopkeepers and property owners were out in those same streets and in that same quiet aftermath, wearing protective coverings of heavy fiber cloth over their bodies as they swept away the dust that remained as the water evaporated.

The brisk sounds of their sweeping added a hollow rhythm to the gait of the *tal* beast.

Tierra Waganat, head of the Waganat Family, fidgeted inside the carriage, his body jostling with a gentle sway as it bounced over the uneven brick path. Despite his distaste for it, he wore his formal council robe, dark Waganat maroon with the proper orange trim. It fit him trimly and carried a sense of respect unto itself. If nothing else the traditional garb gave him a feeling of strength and purpose that he knew he sorely needed.

I am a Waganat, the garment said. *I control my destiny.*

The motion of the carriage annoyed him, though.

Everything annoyed him anymore.

The whole thing—everything from the need for the session in the first place, to the fact that Azat Tegra demanded he come to her Family offices—was annoying.

Still, Tierra Waganat would have climbed to the top of any peak in the Esgarat ring to meet with Azat Tegra if that's what she demanded.

He assumed she knew this.

He'd been able to forestall the worst effects of Baraq's bombing by rallying the Families to search for his brother in the mountains, but that operation had run its course now.

His compound remained shattered, his communication systems—the primary purpose of his Family business—were now mute, and the *hedgie* mercenaries the Waganats had always used to provide security were scattering in the direction of whatever winds would pay them more. He still had stock of equipment to sell, but the Waganats had lost four shops and customers were afraid to enter the rest, and unattended shops were as good as no shops at all.

If Tierra didn't staunch this endless stream of trouble now, one of the Families would try something soon. And if that happened, the Waganat name could fade away as surely as water had dropped under the mountain.

He needed this meeting.

Which made the demand to come to her manor just that much more of a slight.

It said Azat Tegra most certainly did understand the direness in Tierra's situation. That she called the session for the later part of the heat—a moment he was sure she designed to make his travels more public, or at least public enough—added to the burn.

Street traffic or not, the word would seep out.

Tierra Waganat was going to the Tegras.

Everyone would understand what that meant.

It didn't matter, though. Pain or none, Tierra Waganat would do whatever it took to save his Family's position.

I will remember this, though, he thought as he glanced out the open window into the passing street. *I will remember.*

His stomachs rumbled as he watched sweepers taking such pains to avoid what fcw puddles remained.

He scoffed, then wrapped his hand more tightly around the ball of his heavy walking stick that lay across his lap. He felt himself getting wound tighter as thoughts raced through his mind.

Water was water. The time of burning rains had now passed, so there was no longer any reason to fear these waters from the sky.

"Look at them," he said under his breath. "These creatures have no mind for science. The color of the clouds alone should have been enough to say it was safe."

From his place on the opposite side of the carriage, Jee El clicked his sharp affirmative. "They are idiots," he replied.

"Superstition still holds sway over the urchins," Castaada, who sat beside Jee El, added.

The two had been in loyal Waganat employ for many cycles, which is why he'd trusted them to attend with him.

"Superstition will always hold sway over *hedgie* urchins and lesser quadars," Jee said. "Brada should have understood that before he became Lelo and riled up all the troubles."

Tierra clicked more affirmatives.

These sweepers had no mind for truths, hence were unable to determine what was real. They still feared that touching the water would scar them, or at least still feared that their customers feared such a ridiculous outcome. He heard the claims. The calls that some still worried that the gouges and cracks that those burning rains had etched into their buildings would only be made worse.

Which is why the Family structure was so important to All of Esgarat.

Families understood science, and commerce.

It was the combination of the two that had made something as glorious as Esgarat City into the marvel that it was. It was that combination that would ensure its everlasting growth.

So, he stifled a grumble as he watched the sweepers dry their puddles.

At least there were benefits to such ignorance.

Empty streets meant for easy travels.

He glanced at Jee and Castaada. "When we get there," he said, "I need to be the one who speaks."

"We understand," Castaada said.

Jee agreed.

Tierra had considered going alone to the session with Azat Tegra but decided the Family's matriarchal potentate would consider that a signal of weakness—that to travel alone would mean he could not afford to bring such resources with him.

Unfortunately, Azat was correct.

Repairs required after his brother's attack on the Family compound were proceeding with desperate slowness. Castaada and Jee were his two best coordinators, and every day they were gone was another day the Waganat Family was exposed.

Tierra had no other options, though.

These were the only two quadars in his control that he trusted enough to join him on this trek. Since he did not need their counsel, it meant that the two were simply ornamental muscle. If nothing else, though, their presence made him feel better.

The carriage bounced hard enough that Tierra nearly fell from his seat. He groaned, took a deep sigh, and gritted his jaws together. The jolt had run a spike of pain up his back, but he wasn't going to show it to them.

"What will you say?" Jee asked.

Tierra smiled then.

"We will see," he replied. "Won't we?"

The carriage jerked to a halt in front of the Tegra manor, and Tierra pushed the door open. Jee El exited first, then Castaada. They waited for Tierra to exit last. Both his escorts were tall, Jee El broad chested and muscular enough that he looked like someone had wedged him into his formal maroon Waganat uniform.

The soles of their sandals rang on the clean flagstones leading to the expansive and open stairway that rose to the offices of the Tegra Family, marked by a pair of thick columns of carved basalt.

When they arrived at the wide doors, an attendant stepped aside to give passage.

Despite both Jee and Castaada being large quadars, traversing the entryway had its effect of making Tierra feel small. The presence of the two of them served to give Tierra a degree of normality, though. The meat to their bones provided a sense of security he needed to keep calm.

His footsteps echoed against the polished stone of the open

foyer, which was of rounded shape and swept pristinely clean. The sound of water gurgled from a small fountain built into the center of the area.

Ostentatious, yes.

Water was the only resource the council considered a community resource, meaning that they ensured no Family owned its source outright. Indeed, the Families saw it as only good business to co-fund the maintenance of the public system that ensured everyone from the lowest *hedgie* to the top of the Family hierarchy had enough to drink. Still, any quadar who had interest in drilling down to the chasmic rivers deep below could do so. It was pricey, though. And given those arrangements from the council, unnecessary.

Still, the hissing rush of sweet-smelling water heightened the power differential between the Families now.

"Come this way," the Tegra attendant said.

When they came eventually to Azat's office the attendant opened the door and stepped back so Tierra could enter.

It was a large enough space, but smaller than he expected—slightly wider than it was long, the corners rounded rather than squared. A light breeze carried the aroma of *dashtar* citrus over the area, and Tierra's schooled gaze noticed a gravity-fed air system arranged along the far wall.

Azat Tegra sat at the center of her rounded desk, which itself filled the center of the room. The Tegra leader gazed up from a ledger on the desk before her. Her expression said Tierra was interrupting. She hesitated, then motioned to the single chair before her, obviously meant for him.

"Tierra Waganat," she said. "So glad to see you today."

"The pleasure is completely mine."

As Tierra moved to take the seat, Jee and Castaada entered behind him.

"Your enforcers will have to remain outside," Azat said.

"They are reliable."

"Very good to hear," she replied. The skin around her primaries grew tighter. "Still. You may have one quadar in the room for this conversation. I leave it to you to determine who that one quadar is."

The tilt of her head told Tierra she wasn't joking.

"Wait outside," he said to his escorts.

They had spoken of the potential for Tegra treachery prior to arriving, and for an instant Tierra wasn't sure they were going to comply, but then Jee moved and the tension broke.

"Let us know if you need anything," Jee said, turning a quick stare to Azat.

"I will."

A moment later the door shut, and they were alone.

Tierra adjusted himself on the seat Azat provided.

Azat was a formidable presence in all circumstances, but today she seemed three sizes bigger than he ever recalled. She had led the Tegra Family for as long as Tierra could remember, and though older than most quadars she was still muscular and still trim in the way that made her clothes seem to fit perfectly no matter what she wore, which today was a deep red pullover upper, and a pair of knee-length trousers made of tanned skin. She sat upright in her seat, alert and surrounded by the flat plane of the table that, from this angle, appeared to wrap completely around her.

A scattered collection of what appeared to be financial sheets covered the desk. The remnants of her lunch sat on a tray far to her left, a half-eaten *hoi* root the only identifiable scrap.

Her chair loomed higher than his.

She gazed at him for several beats, giving Tierra ample time to take in the three branded scars that angled down her right cheekbone to demark her as Family Tegra and Clan Terilamat.

Scarification was an element of the Terilamat tradition that his own house had forsaken over the past few generations. Barbaric, he'd say if he were on his own. But the Tegras practiced the old ways, and the intense judgment of her gaze made the smooth skin of his own face feel uncomfortable.

"So," she said, raising her brow and allowing her central to come open just a bit farther. "I understand the Waganat clan is in some trouble."

"Nothing we can't handle with a little effort."

"That is good to hear," Azat replied.

She returned to scanning her sheets, then.

After a moment she made a small grunt, then reached for a writing instrument to make a mark on one of the pages.

"Excuse me," Tierra said.

She looked up.

"I thought we were talking about how we might help each other," he said.

"Oh," Azat replied with a passive expression. "I'm so sorry. I thought you said the Waganats were able to handle things on your own."

Tierra felt it then, the cold essence of what it meant to be the hunted rather than the hunter.

She put the writing instrument down with a calm precision, then turned back to Tierra, folding her long fingers together before leaning against the edge of the table.

"Tell me then, Tierra Waganat. What do you want?"

He smiled and leaned forward to get to business.

"We both know that the seams are coming apart around the city. You have weapons. We have communications. I want to make a pact that, combined, will make us the most important organization in All of Esgaral."

"And why would I do that?"

"Your guns are no good unless you know where to point them."

"Your technology is gone."

"But my networks are still good, and our knowledge is intact. Given proper time I can rebuild the stocks."

Azat sat in stoic silence for long enough that discomfort built. "It must be very hard," she finally said.

"What is that?"

"Your father was a rock for the Waganat Family."

"Yes," Tierra replied. "He was."

He brushed his hand down one thigh.

"But he has returned to the Mountain."

"Yes," Tierra said. "He's dead."

"And your brother has destroyed the foundation your entire Family was based on."

"What is your point?"

"That must be a hard position to be in," she said, her gaze softening in a way that raised hackles along Tierra's back. Azat Tegra slowly sat backward and absently ran a fingertip over the scars on her cheek. "You are a young, more modern version of your father, full of his ambition and bravado. I see that, Tierra. Sincerely I do. But now—just as you get your hands on the controls—

everything you own is rocked from beneath you."

Tierra fought the urge to blink.

How much did the Tegra Family know about their true situation?

Ranya Waganat had once held a stranglehold on communications within and around the city—something that came with the invention of their wave talkers and had entrenched their Family into society. But Tierra's father exercised that power with measures that were sometimes more stern than they needed to be. So stern that Tierra's first act upon taking his father's seat at the Council of Clans had been to send a very public Jee around to every subordinate clan's business to assure them that nothing had changed—that the Waganats would meet any missed payments of proper license fees with unpleasant responses.

All was well until Lelo revealed himself to be a Waganat, which raised questions among Tierra's clientele.

Baraq's attack had ensured that the rest fell apart from there.

"Confronting Lelo as you did seems to have been a mistake," Azat said.

"We did only what we had to. Baraq should have seen that," Tierra said.

"Your brother was always wiser than he let on."

"I wouldn't say that."

"I don't really care what you would say, Tierra."

Tierra braced himself with his walking stick and stood.

"I don't need to take this," he said. His hearts were pumping now. Heat pooled in his shoulder plates. "I didn't come here to be insulted."

"No, you did not come here to be insulted," Azat said in a coldly calm voice. "You came here to pretend that you still have value, even though you do not. You came here to pretend your network of *hedgies* is still feeding you intelligence when it clearly is not. You came here, for some unknown reason, in hopes I might offer you a deal at discount. So, no, Tierra Waganat, you didn't come here to be insulted. You came here to insult me—you came here to pretend you are stronger than you are in hopes that I would give you an arrangement that would save your Family."

It took every bit of strength Tierra had to not fall back into the seat he stood before. It took every bit of his humility to take a breath and then ease himself back into that seat.

He gazed at her, taking in the set of her face, and realized this was why she had sent Jee and Castaada out of the room. With them gone there were no witnesses to his flaying. With no witnesses, there was a chance to go onward.

The idea was the only thing that gave him the strength to continue.

"All right," he said. "What do you want?"

Azat put her hands together.

"Everything you have," she said. "I want it all."

CHAPTER 5

It was time, Ezi Waganat thought as she stared at flames that flickered from the pit at the center of the cave's dark opening. Their wavering light illuminated the highest points of each leader's face as they sat in their place in the circle.

Heat rose up the mountainside.

Cool air came from the passage's depths.

It was nearing full darktime, and clouds were forming along the distant ridgeline. For the first time since the group arrived here Ezi thought it might rain.

She steeled herself.

Brada, her pair-mate, was dead. Baraq, her *dada*—her pair-mate's father—was gone missing in the mountain, which meant he, too, was probably dead. The *hedgie* population that comprised the bulk of their resources were scattered—soon to be gathered up in the growing storm of Family War that loomed on the horizon as certainly as if it were one of those dark clouds.

The group had needed time to gather themselves, which is why they'd come here in the first place.

But it was time.

So, for the first time since they had arrived at the shelter, the scraps that remained of the Orange Ring had agreed to gather in leadership ring around the fire.

From her place in the circle, she took them in, feeling a fresh wave of grief at Brada's absence. Ezi didn't know if she could lead the group. Didn't know if they would accept her or find someone else. In truth, she didn't care if it was her or not. All she felt as she sat preparing to begin again was that she would do anything it took to honor Brada's life, and the best thing she knew to do now was to continue to follow his work.

After the massacre, the Orange Ring had retreated into the higher regions of the foothills to this place, known as Nectani Gap, an abandoned network of craggy passages named for the long-passed family that had lived here for generations.

The caves had been an outpost in the earliest days of Ezi's life, a place large enough to house a few small families and with a natural ventilation that brought cooler air up from the depths. Generations earlier, residents had cut crannies into the gap large enough to store dry root and other necessities, which had probably been useful at some point. Several heats trying to live here had shown Ezi its possibilities, but nothing could hide the fact that the arca around it was now barren, that even the *havra* root that had once thrived in the shadowed grounds opposite the tall cliffs nearby had been burned dry by the combination of direct heatfall and the burning waters that had fallen so heavily from the sky.

Over the cycles Nectani Gap had been used mostly as nomadic campgrounds by the free rangers who would pass through it on their way to other destinations.

Now she knew why they passed through and didn't settle here.

But, while life had been uncomfortable since they'd arrived, the place had given them what they needed when they needed it most—distance from Esgarat City, and freedom from the Families.

Ezi was preparing to open the session when Brother Fali Notash spoke.

"We are finished," he said. "Without Lelo, there is no reason to go on."

"No," Ezi replied too quickly. She pressed her lips together and used the awkwardness of the moment to take in the other faces around the circle. There were eight of them—nine if you counted little Pella, who was seated on a pile of fiber straw against the distant cave wall, watching them with eyes wide.

Some had argued the whelpling was too young to be here, but Ezi wanted to keep her engaged.

She has done her part in the struggle, Ezi argued. *She's earned her pillow against the wall.*

After the moment settled, in which the only sound was the fire crackling and the only smell was the coarse smoke that came from the smoldering of thick root, Ezi spoke again.

"You have been a fierce member of the Ring, Brother Fali. I do not mean to reduce the value of your views. But I note that you have been a member of this leadership ring for only a cycle, and I do not think you are right to say we are finished."

"We've all seen the destruction," Fali replied. "We've all seen the dead."

"Of course we have," Ezi replied. "But I am not ready to give up."

The postures around the circle showed mixed reaction.

"This moment is why I called the session," she said. "And the question Fali raises is not an unwise question. We cannot sustain a life here in this place with no easy food or water—that much is true, and to be clear, I do not want to sustain a life here. I want to live in the Esgarat City of our dreams. I want to live in a place where all quadars can live, where all quadars can love and thrive in the ways they wish to."

"As was Brada's vision," Vareta, the elder of their numbers, said.

"We cannot win," Fali replied.

"I am Brada's pair-mate. I say otherwise."

"You *were* Brada's pair-mate," Fali interjected.

Ezi let the attack burn inside her for an instant so that she did not lash out.

"There is no call for that," Vareta said, giving her more time.

"It is all right, Sister," Ezi said, holding a hand up to gather attention. She turned to take on Fali's firm gaze. The young quadar was anxious now, she saw. Defeated and defensive.

"You are right, Fali Notash. I cannot blame you for noting that I *was* Brada's pair-mate. And you are right that I have seen his death, too. I saw it up close, and I have seen it over and over again, every night as it plays out in the images of my sleep. But other things play in my sleep, too. Brada's ideas come to me unbidden. His directions to love each other. His ideas of what it means to give every whelpling like our own little Pella a good life. These things are there in my sleeps because I have also seen Brada's vision up close. Because I was there for every decision this group made, even in the days when it was just a small group of quadars who found ways to share *havra* bread with the *hedgies* and the lesser families."

She stopped there.

Waiting.

Examining Fali Notash with her inquisitive expression.

"I am sorry," Fali replied. He rubbed the flesh of his cheeks with one hand. "I'm just..." he said. "I'm very tired."

He breathed deeply then, his chest wracking with his exhale.

"It's all right."

The fire crackled. Then Ezi continued.

"That's the question at hand, though, is it not? Whether Brada's vision is to ever become real. Fali's despair is one we've all shared. It's natural to need this time to gather our feelings, and I cannot deny that I, too, have had moments where I felt Fali's sense of doom."

"I have, too," Oast'el, the ranking member of the Orange Army and once one of Brada's closest friends, said in the moment Ezi left open.

She waited, then, waited as she felt Brada would have.

Oast'el continued. "I've denied certain facts, then argued in my mind about who should carry certain responsibilities for our failure."

"Of which there are many," Vareta added.

Ezi glanced around the circle.

"Is there any among us who has not had those thoughts?"

No one replied.

"So, they are good to have, are they not? These questions are good. We retreated to these foothills as much to debate these questions as to mourn our losses, and I suggest to you as the darktime creeps upon us that for us, those two things are even the same things. We cannot mourn our losses without questioning our purposes."

"So, what would you have us do?" Fali Notash replied after several beats.

Ezi's hearts soared.

"I cannot say yet. Other than to ask us each to see the world differently."

"Differently?"

"To my way of seeing things the vision we all share has not changed. Nor has the world. But until now the Orange Ring has been playing a game in which we did not acknowledge the rules. We met together in sessions like this one, posturing about how the world *should* be, convincing ourselves through the hubris of intellect that a steady and stable connection to the quadars who did the work, and the mere presentation of facts that were so obvious to each of us, would be all it took to change the world around us."

Heads nodded sideways and back as Ezi spoke.

They were settling in. She was gaining momentum.

"This was the frame Brada himself fostered, and it made sense to us because this was the same Brada who was son of Baraq and—before he pulled his mask down to reveal himself—who had been known to the world as Lelo. He fired these quadars' minds with our ideas of freedom and prosperity and the ability to lead a good life. He had built a following willing to die for it.

"Yet none of us were ready for the carnage the Families brought upon us. None of us predicted the bloodshed that was now so predictable in retrospect."

"I think this is right," Vareta said.

"We know better now, though, don't we," Ezi said. "The Families have revealed their full natures, and now that we've exposed their depravity, we cannot let those natures define the vision for all quadars of the future. While those natures define the chore that stands before us, we cannot leave them to stand on their own."

Ezi felt it then. The shift.

The sense of anticipation that had grown over the gathering.

Time had moved on, and from here in the relative safety of the protected hillsides, the Orange Ring was coming to the point where they were ready to act again.

"It is time," Ezi said.

More heads nodded.

"You can each feel it, too, can you not? This is what Brada would say to us if he were still here now. That now is the time to return to the city, now is the time to engage with the lesser families again, to help the quadars that we cultivated for so long. Because now is the time they are in their greatest need. The city is crumbling, which makes for dangerous moments, but also gives opportunity.

The Families have shown their true natures. It is time to show ours."

Oast'el, the ranking member of the Orange Army, spoke up.

"Yes," he said. "I do feel that."

"I agree that is what Brada would be telling us," Vareta added. "Though my hearts are still heavy. He would want us to persist."

"So what do we do?" Oast'el said.

The rest, including Fali Notash, edged forward.

Ezi set her bearing.

"No one here—least of all, me—is Brada. Believe me when I say that I know this better than any of us. I think these actions need to be group discussions. So I propose we adjourn for now, that each of us consider options we think are positive. Then return to the circle to discuss those ideas at next heat."

"That sounds wise," Vareta said.

When no one dissented, Ezi brought the gathering to a close.

"All right, then," she said, standing. "Enjoy your sleeps."

In the distance, the sky flashed, and the sound of thunder rumbled over All of Esgarat.

CHAPTER 6

Baraq Waganat picked his way along the shadows cast by Esgarat City's tallest buildings, his soft-sandaled feet striding silently over its hard-packed streets.

He was tired from his travels. His body ached, and his thoughts danced from one piece of his plan to avenge his son's death to the next. If he'd had time Baraq would have waited another few heats simply to recuperate, but time was short.

He needed a weapon now, though.

So, he made his way through these familiar streets toward the Tegra storehouse, shadows deepening as he progressed.

He thought first of Brada, then Ezi, his son's *kalla* and equal in her role with the Orange Army.

Ezi, and what remained of that group, would have wanted Baraq to come to them upon his arrival in the city. He could have found them if he wanted to. His son had built his network honestly. It would not be hard to find them.

But he did not want to join with them.

His failure to acquire the high-powered weapons he'd wanted from Louratna's community meant he had nothing to give to the Orange Ring but his blood, and that had proven to be worth less than he liked to think. Without the force of those weapons behind them, the Orange Ring would be mostly defenseless against the Families.

He thought about Louratna, too.

And wondered if the creature named Torranze still lived, or if it, too, had been murdered by the Families. He'd heard nothing, so he couldn't be sure.

As he strode down the central street now, the city spoke to him with familiar sounds and with familiar odors from shops that clotted the air as it flowed in the artificial caverns of its taller buildings. He could taste despair here. Whispered breezes filled his ears with ragged noise. A dilapidated motor cart puttered down the road in the opposite direction of his walking, a pair of mercenary security soldiers sprawled over the platform at its back.

Less traffic filled the streets than usual.

Shoppers were scarce, and what few were there scampered from stall to stall rather than strolled between them, leaving each vendor close-lipped and without remark, their transactions and bartering made with sharp efficiency. They hovered closer to the protective sides of buildings that loomed over them, too, as if pretending the walls could guard against what was coming.

Several businesses had already closed their doors early.

Quadars were on edge.

Even the *hedgies*, invisible to most, seemed to huddle more deeply into their dark nooks, their roaming gangs of street urchins—normally full of chatter and bravado—were now quietly murmuring in their pleas.

As he crossed over a path, his foot kicked a small rock that then skittered loudly across the brick street. Alert gazes came his way, and Baraq fought the urge to pull his hood even further over his face.

He had left that hood up in a fashion acceptable because such coverings claimed to keep the black rot at bay. Baraq had seen what the rot could do, but all that mattered to him now was that the hood served as cover. Baraq couldn't afford for his face to be recognized now.

In this way, the lighter coloring of the robe was purposeful, too. Though Baraq did not want to be *recognized*, he did want to be *seen*, and the best place to hide was in plain sight.

He walked in the open so that the obvious nature of his presence became a statement.

Pace was important, too—steady and controlled—a gait that said he had a place to be, a reason to walk the street that wasn't with devious intention.

He was simply heading home.

Merely leaving the districts of commerce to make his long trek back to some nondescript hovel where he would continue to eke out his meager existence.

Nothing here to see.

He crossed over the street and continued the path toward the setting heats.

His plan was to slip into the back of the Tegra storehouse, gather as many munitions as he could carry, then set a few well-timed fuses and get out.

As an ex-member of the Council of Clans, Baraq knew the Tegras would not make it easy. They were a strong Family. A Family that bought and sold arms under an exclusive charter given by that same council.

Back when he was a shopkeeper, Baraq had owned one of their weapons, a small gun that fit into one palm—before his father had ordered Baraq to divest himself of it, anyway, and had placed other restrictions on him for his mishandling of the Light That Fell from the Sky. His brother had finally made that order stick by taking the gun from him during Baraq's ill-fated first attempt at killing that same father.

Azat Tegra—that Family's matriarchal leader—was a sharp-witted businessperson with no patience for subtext. She was an opportunist, able to smell both blood and water from a horizon away.

She was also no fool.

She would sense the upcoming war between the Families.

She would already be planning for ways to leverage her position in Terilamat clan as they looked to defend themselves against the Hlrat and Kandar clans.

She would see, in other words, the multilayered complexities such a war would bring—pieces of clans warring with each other, but collectives matching up to protect the greater victory at hand.

She would understand the shift that was already underway inside the city's power systems, and she would realize that Baraq had brought his Waganat Family to its knees—the Waganats, one of the most powerful of all Families—and she would then calculate all the ramifications that these facts brought to bear.

Azat Tegra would see the Waganat Family was vulnerable—indeed, it wouldn't surprise him if she had made plans for the possibility some time ago.

The Tegra defenses would be on alert.

His time on the council had given him a small advantage, though. It was simple good fortune that he'd been at the right place to take in a whispered conversation between young Bella Tegra and the Banit whelp she fancied.

Baraq understood immediately the young couple's need for secrecy. The Banit Family may be well-positioned, but the coarse nature of their farmland origins and their association as Kandar clan would make for difficult conversations within the Tegra compound.

The Tegra were Terilamat, and staunchly Terilamat at that.

Azat would look harshly on any pairing outside the clan.

It was through that whispered conversation that Baraq had learned the existence of another entrance to the storehouse—a secret one that would be hidden in the shadows of the evening, a trap door down into the stores where the Tegra family would host the business meetings they wanted to protect from the eyes of the council, or, Baraq thought for a wistful moment, where youthful Bella Tegra and her young lover from the Banit Family could tryst.

The secret gate lay behind a hedgerow.

If he could make it to the gate, Baraq was sure he could slip in.

The fact that he was on his own gave him the same advantages that the little *piela* lizard had over the greater *jah.*

He hoped the Tegra guards would overlook him. Still, he had to be careful. His glance at the building, which was three stories and covered in a creeping vine, told him what he needed to know: Three guards out front, two more at the flank, and another two in the back that he could see.

There would be more he couldn't see.

As expected, he would need a diversion.

His lip twisted upward with a smile that carried a certain sense of satisfaction. The Festia Family building was nearby.

Two for one, he thought.

The best kind of revenge.

CHAPTER 7

By the time Baraq slipped into a narrow alley between ramshackle huts, the sky had grown toward full dark. He shouldered his cloak off, revealing tighter clothes underneath, then wadded the robe to carry it in one hand.

Turning sideways, Baraq used the narrow space between the cutlery shop owned by the Pew'tal Family—a lesser business leader in the structures—and the metalsmith co-operative run by Aliander Festia, a quadar of the same Family that Crissandr, Baraq's pairmate, had come from.

An odor of disuse filled the gap between the buildings.

Acrid dust from evaporated rain mixed with scat from random *piela* lizards and their prey that would come out in the morning hours to find scraps of food. The walls, built of rough mudbrick, were cooler than those that faced outward to the street, but they still radiated heat as the nighttime air cooled. Their abrasive surface felt coarse against his back and against his fingertips as he pressed against it.

At least the chill would serve to cool his own blood, hence make him less visible to prying centrals.

That was another advantage of the light-colored robe, too. It had reflected more heat than it absorbed, meaning his body temperature wasn't as elevated as it might have been otherwise. Keeping his heat signature closer to that of the building wouldn't save him from nearby observers, but at this distance he didn't think the Tegra guards would make his profile.

Baraq focused on his plan.

Aliander Festia was young. New to operations.

Quadars around the city—and more important, quadars on the council—would be predisposed to believe he might make a mistake and forget to douse a firepot, which might then lead to a smoldering remnant, which then might catch fire. Any delay in assigning true blame would help.

Aliander also had the Festia tendency to leave his shop unlocked—a practice that some Festia Family members took pride in because they felt it gave them an aura of superiority, as if to say that they were too big to steal from. Too important to cause problems with.

That sense of superiority was a reason Crissandr had chosen to leave her Festia Family to join Baraq's. The Waganat Family was no better in reality, but at least they were not so smug about it.

He pushed thoughts of Crissandr aside.

Making his way, Baraq recalled his father's musings on Festia bravado. Baraq had been mocking the practice of leaving doors unlocked, but Ranya Waganat admonished him. Ranya liked the idea in theory, or at least he admired the thought behind it. It made sense enough for the Festias, Ranya Waganat had said. Their metalworking specialty required unique skills and equipment that was difficult to cart away. The expertise in dealing with liquid fuels that burned hotly enough to make the chemistry of metalworking operate was rare. For the Festia Family, losses to renegade theft would be no more than a few tools here or there—or, in the case of any who stole more, the investigations required to find culprits would not be so difficult.

The Festias were strong enough to deal with looters.

And brutal enough to send messages when they did deal with such looters.

The overhead of enforcement was unlikely to be particularly large for them, though the benefits of the few times it was necessary were worth it.

The Waganat empire was different, though.

Ranya Waganat's foundation was built on wave talkers and surveillance equipment—too many products so easy for any quadar off the street to use made for too many temptations.

Baraq's father liked the statement the Festias were making but didn't want to deal with the headaches that enforcement of such a practice would cost the Waganats.

"Someone steals, and suddenly we have to pay an arm and a leg to send a message?" Ranya Waganat once said between bites of a meal. *"Sounds like too much trouble for us."*

As Baraq made his way to the end of the alleyway, he realized it didn't matter what his father had thought of the Festia practice. The only question that mattered now was whether the coming war between the Families might have already changed the calculus he'd been using. Had things gotten so tense that young Aliander Festia chose to—or, more likely, was directed to—lock his door?

He paused as a skipper board rambled down the street behind him. The wall's coarseness ground against his shoulder plates.

As he edged further down the gap between the buildings, the tunnel ahead gave Baraq a line of sight to a Tegra guard post some distance away. He tensed as two agents came together, then relaxed as they parted.

Calm, he thought as his gaze went to the still-quiet security post. He pressed himself again against the wall at his back.

Remain calm.

He edged further down the alleyway until he reached the front walkway, each halting step coming with a soft rush of fabric on brick that sent his imagination whirling.

With a single movement he went to the metal shop's door, reached to the latch, and was pleasantly encouraged when the door did, indeed, click open.

One question answered.

Baraq slipped quickly into the shop, then shut the door behind.

He was familiar with the shop's basic layout.

His central picked up heat spectrum from counters and tables that still radiated remnants of the operator's work earlier in the day, from brick-lined forges that still burned hot, from areas of the floor where body heat from the clerks and shoppers were still faint splotches on the floor.

Stepping through the room, Baraq opened flue-vents to the outside, then rolled fueling bulbs gently to soak the wicks before he lit the burn pits once again.

Once each fire was burning, he dropped his robe into the largest one. It sizzled with a quick billow of smoke that filled the air.

He went to the storage room then and found more kindling root and mats of rolled fabric used to pad certain pieces.

The kindling he scattered across the main floor and then over the counters, the fabric he wedged into spaces around the counters.

Also from storage, he rolled out large decanters of sloshing, bitter-smelling fuel. Bins of polish, too—buckets of pitchy, viscous material used to bring a shine to their larger pieces of work that would fetch the best prices. These, too, he spilled down onto the floor.

The work was not difficult, but it was taxing.

When he finished, the shop was warm.

His chest heaved with exertion and his eyes burned from smoke and perspiration. He felt the pores of his skin opening to give his body more surface area. The dry heats of the now-blasting forges smelled rich and ready.

Outside the streets were growing full dark.

Settling himself, Baraq pulled a single twisted piece of kindling from the floor, dangled its fringe into the fire, and then lifted its flaming wand. Then, walking again to the door, Baraq dropped the brand onto the fire bed behind him.

The flames jumped quickly from bit to bit.

Fabric began to smolder.

Thin trails of smoke formed curling waves that roiled against the walls.

As Baraq left the building, a few wisps filtered out from the set of flues to curl into the nighttime sky.

By the time he arrived back near the Tegra storehouse, smoke rose over a roof across the way. A few moments later, a fire bell rang.

Now racing away, Baraq let his gaze go to the Tegra mansion where the guards turned to take in the sight of the Festia metal shop bursting into flames.

CHAPTER 8

As smoke roiled from the Festia shop, Baraq hunched in a darkened recess, behind a ramshackle cart that sat across the dirt-lined street from the Tegra manor. He'd have to be quick but being alone gave him certain advantages.

The voice of a guard called across the looming darkness. Other guards came to join him.

The quadar pointed toward the cloud of smoke that was now billowing from the metal shop. All three paused to take it in.

The odor of fire came stronger.

"Go," one called, pushing their mate forward to explore.

A second followed, limping with some uncertain ailment.

The cloud of smoke darkened the sky enough that it blocked the emerging starlight above the buildings.

More voices came from the distance.

Baraq's gaze went to a row of dry, shadow-draped hedge brush that ran along the rear of the storehouse. His information said the passage into the weapon stores would be just beyond that. If he had remembered the conversation correctly, the doorway would lever upward.

A full tongue of flame burst from the metal shop's window, and a dull explosion whumped through the night, drawing the guards' full attention.

Now! Baraq thought, hearts pounding.

He hunched down and raced forward, using the cart as cover for as long as he could. His legs burned as he crossed the path with controlled haste. The hedgerow was tall enough he could almost stand upright as he slinked further along the building.

The odor of smoke grew sharp, and more voices raised.

Baraq's hearts pounded with acidic fear.

Be quick, he told himself, *but don't hurry.*

He nearly jumped for delight to come to the pair of double doors that angled downward. He'd heard true. The crevasse was there between those doors, too—a finger-width gap that should lead him to the levers.

Perfect.

He ran a finger slowly down the channel, hearing the calls and the heavy footfall of quadars racing to the fire. Each moment his search came up empty, he thought his hearts might burst.

There.

A trigger.

He pushed it and heard the low grind of gearing groan from underneath. The sound worried him, but a glance at the guard stand showed they remained focused on the fire across the way.

A moment later the door wedged half open.

Stone slabbed stairs led into inky darkness.

Baraq pulled the door further upward and slipped quickly into the void. Then he levered the door back into place and let his central take in the stairwell.

To his left was a rail.

The steps were wide, and easy to descend.

Moving quickly, he followed them into darkness.

As his central grew familiar with the room's thin heat signature, he realized he was in a small storeroom filled with shovels, rakes, and other gardening tools the Tegra used to maintain the manor. An open doorway led to a squared-off tunnel cut down to the basement, with openings on each side. Down the way, a faint line of light glowed from the outline of a door.

Muffled sounds came from the opposite side.

More security, Baraq realized.

Coming his way, drawn by the creaking of the door engines.

Instinctively, Baraq raced toward the door, trying to remain silent but hearing the calamitous sound of his own breathing and afraid that the pounding of his feet on the floor were as loud as drums beating at full power.

He had to get to the door, though.

Whatever advantage he had was gone the moment they found him. He had to take care of this now, before everything got away from him.

The doorway swung away from him.

Light splayed into the hallway revealing a form there, a guard, Baraq saw.

Leaping before he fully took the situation in, Baraq used his fist to strike the guard with a solid crunch, taking the sentry high on the crown as the quadar gave a stunted cry.

A weapon clattered to the floor.

The two hit the ground in a pile, the guard's head impacting with a sickening crunch.

Baraq bent over him, panting, and ready to pummel the quadar again if needed. But the guard's primaries were glazed over and dilating, his central snapped shut. He was breathing, but unconscious.

A flash of desperate anger seared him.

He hadn't wanted to hurt anyone, partially because he didn't like the idea of it all, but just as much because he didn't want to give the Tegras anything so personal to respond to.

Baraq clenched his jaw and fought the urge to punch the wall. His neck gave a twitch.

Maybe the guard would recover.

He rose, though. Noting the awkwardly limp posture of the quadar and replaying the sound of skull against floor, it didn't bode well.

His chest constricted.

It was too late for this kind of thinking. No use shedding water over the past.

Just get in and get out, he thought.

A rack against one wall held rows of long-barreled guns. Smaller weapons filled a cabinet of cubbyholes built below the racks. A long table held a new type of gun—one he hadn't seen before, anyway. Four barrels welded together, each with their own firing mechanism.

Multiple rounds, he thought.

Four guns' worth of firepower in one weapon.

He noted a strap looped from its stock to its midpoint.

Crates of ammunition covered a solid, sturdy table in the middle of the room. His gaze flitted around the room. No fuses. No bombs.

Damn.

Without explosives, he wouldn't be able to destroy the storeroom.

He checked on the guard below him again.

The quadar was semiconscious but senseless, mouth gaping open as if trying to say something, but clearly unable.

"Onjay?" a voice came from somewhere a distance away.

Baraq glanced in that direction, toward another closed door.

He guessed that the door opened to another corridor, and from the sounds he figured it was a stairway upward—toward the main area of the Tegra offices.

How many more guards were up there?

How quickly could they get down here?

Any answer greater than zero was bad news.

Time slowed.

He got to work, moving swiftly but surely.

He grabbed the four-shooter and looped the strap over his shoulder. Pulled a gun from a cubby and jammed it into a pocket. Another went into his waist belt. From the table he scooped three crates of ammunition into one arm and grabbed one more in the opposite hand.

Footsteps rambled.

"Onjay?

The voice was closer now.

Baraq slipped out of the weapons room and yanked the door closed behind him. He raced back down the hallway he had come from.

The gun in his waist belt shifted, and his chest nearly exploded with fear that it was going to slip out and clatter against the stone walls of the passage.

It stayed in place, though.

Instead, it was the four-shooter, bouncing back and forth on the strap, that crashed against the wall, the barrels ringing like bells as he ran. Then, as he reached back with his one hand to steady the weapon, one of the ammunition crates slipped from his grip to rain a cascading river of bullets across the floor behind him.

So much for stealth.

No longer trying to hide his presence, Baraq clambered up the stairs.

Voices and the heavy falling of footsteps came from the hallway behind. As he arrived at the trap door, the doorway to the weapons storeroom behind him opened and flooded the hallway with light again.

Calmly Baraq crammed his now-free hand into the trap door's lever system, then—as the door began to move—pressed his feet against the upper steps and shoved his shoulder against the door to augment its gearing.

The door gave way with the thick metallic grate of gears shredding themselves. Baraq's extra push threw it open.

He stumbled forward with unexpected release, falling against the rocky manor hard enough to scrape the skin of his exposed hand and crash a shin into a sharp edge of the stairwell that descended below.

Behind him footsteps neared the stairs.

With no time to check his injuries, he scampered, limping down the path he'd come from, one arm still cradling the two remaining crates, the other going from trying to control the four-shooter that jostled back and forth in his wake to holding onto the smaller gun he'd stored in his waist belt.

The smell of the fire from the Festia shop was intense, now.

The sound of the city responding was a wall of voices and animal groans. Every bit of his anxiety wanted to turn to see if Tegra guards had come through the trap door, but he didn't let himself.

Instead, he ran.

As hard as he could.

He turned the corner to race behind the tall hedgerow. His hearts pounded. His chest felt like it was going to explode. The handgun slipped from its holder, and Baraq grabbed it quickly. Empty weapon in one hand, the other still balancing crates of bullets, he raced across the pitch-dark street and then down a row that was home to three other businesses.

The sound of pursuit was distant, but there.

He ducked into an alleyway where he'd hidden a dilapidated skipper board he'd found and repaired earlier in the day. He knocked off some dirt and flipped it right side up. Turning the small electric motor on, he stepped gingerly on board. It wouldn't go far, but he didn't need range now. All he cared about was the relative silence the vehicle would provide.

The pain in his shin came as he waited for the motor to spin up—sharp, but not so bad as to keep him from moving.

The aroma of the motor warming filtered up to him.

Balancing the crates and leaning against the skipper board's handles, he hit the throttle. The vehicle shot forward with enough of a jerk he almost lost his balance.

The alleyway was broader than the gap between buildings he'd passed through earlier. A corner loomed ahead. Behind, the sound of gunfire roared, and a shard of the wall beside him exploded.

Baraq ducked and leaned into a hard turn.

A moment later he was in the clear.

Two moments later he'd banked into a new turn and then a new alleyway. Several turns later, he dumped the skipper board, and—still clutching his weapons and ammunition tightly—made his way on foot, disappearing into the darkness.

It was only then—after he knew he was safe and after things had calmed—that he realized he was bleeding from a cut above his cheekbone.

A piece of the building, he thought.

Or perhaps a shard from the bullet had cut him.

It was then, only then, despite having gained the weapons he carried now, that he felt the hollowness inside his hearts and realized the true depths of his disappointment.

The Tegra storehouse was still standing.

Anger welled inside him. He had succeeded this darktime, but his success hadn't been enough. Hadn't even begun to dent the pain of watching Brada be murdered by the Families. Perhaps, he thought, nothing would ever be enough.

He pressed against the wound at his forehead, and made his way silently down the streets, to the edges of the city, tasting this new sense of certainty that came to him in the darkness.

He felt the past in his tired body.

He felt the future in the trickle of blood that ran down his cheeks.

In putting them together Baraq knew only one thing.

He wanted to hurt the Families.

No. That wasn't correct, he thought as his grip pressed harder against the gun. He didn't want to hurt the Families. He wanted to destroy them.

CHAPTER 9

The sound of mallets rang across the entire Waganat compound. Voices rose and fell. Though the heat was still early, Tierra Waganat had no time to lose. As he scanned the tangled piles of wire and brick strewn across the compound, the smells of freshly exposed soil and open breeze made his stomachs burn.

The city around him felt too close.

He cringed at the sensation of prying primaries even if he could not see them.

Esgarat City did not allow for weakness. Only the fact of the Waganat name had kept them safe from anything beyond petty theft so far.

"When will this be cleaned out?" he said as he pressed his heavy walking stick into the ground to step over one of the tangled masses of foundation and wire that littered the compound.

Jee El followed in his wing position, a half-step behind and to his left, walking with heavier steps than Tierra.

Though he was not a born Waganat, Jee wore the classic loose gray shirts and billowing pants of the Waganat clan, trimmed in red thread as their tradition called for. He clasped his hands behind his back.

"Soon now, Master Waganat," he responded. "The workers we are receiving from the Tegras are arriving in larger numbers each heat. Progress will grow more rapid."

Tierra grunted approval as they came upon a *hedgie* who was unloading brick squares from a newly arrived allotment.

Those bricks, too, were a value that came from the deal he'd made. Azat Tegra still had the leverage to clear administrative hurdles that he did not now possess. She had expedited the brick load to him ahead of others. The price had been dear, but Azat Tegra had been good to her word so far. Taking account of that leverage—the weaponry that hung from his Waganat guards' belts and the influx of *hedgie* labor suddenly available to him—he knew it had been worth it.

"I want this wall complete before Eldoro down," Tierra said to the *hedgie.*

"I can only do what can be done," the *hedgie* replied.

Tierra's walking stick struck the quadar before he even knew it was coming.

The *hedgie* raised his hand as a shield. "I'm sorry, Master Waganat."

"Eldoro down," Tierra reiterated in a firm, monotone voice. "Do you hear me? I want this wall completed by Eldoro down. If you didn't appreciate the tap I provided, I'm sure you'll find the things my compatriot does to quadars who do not complete their tasks on time to be considerably less enjoyable."

Beside him, Jee stood without motion, but still managed to flex a muscle.

The *hedgie* bent to pick up more brickwork.

"Come, Jee," Tierra finally said. "We have items to discuss."

Tierra stepped across the mess.

They were surveying the Waganat compound—ostensibly so Tierra could inspect repairs and the rebuilds across the Family grounds, but mostly because Tierra wanted to ensure the content of the discussion remained private.

Among the technologies he had given away were a number of their smallest wave talkers and several other pieces of surveillance equipment. Given that the Waganat compound still stood wide open, Tierra found it best to assume Azat had found a way to infiltrate his office, so it was only prudent to assume Azat Tegra was aware of every discussion of importance made inside that office.

He found it ironic that only by speaking out here in the open could they do so without fear of being overheard.

"Your agreement seems to have paid off," Jee said as they walked.

"It is too early to get complacent," Tierra replied.

The arrangement left the Tegras in prime position to control Esgarat City, and that could cause problems farther down the path, but Tierra knew better than any other quadar exactly how deep his Family's troubles ran.

"I'm sorry to be so hasty."

"Think nothing of it, my friend," Tierra said, giving a lilting bit of a chuckle. "In truth it's nice to be able to think that."

"No, you were right to begin with. There is still a lot to go wrong."

Tierra clicked agreement.

"You don't know half of it."

"I'm sure I do not."

Stepping carefully, Tierra made his way over a layer of stone that had once been the farthest eastward corner of the manor.

His father had built this section when he was still young—back when he'd first taken the reins of the Family business. That manor had meant something larger to him than just a building. Tierra recalled his father taking strolls like Tierra himself was doing now, but instead of admiring the sturdy nature of the building, all Tierra could do was grimace. Baraq's bombing had leveled the entire structure—only a few jagged teeth of walls still reached up toward the cloudless sky. Several other buildings in the compound—which had been one of the largest in All of Esgarat—had suffered such damage, too.

An errant gust of wind brought the scent of charred brick.

Baraq is going to pay for this, he thought, choking on the odor. *I should have killed him when I had the chance.*

He coughed in a cloud of dust that rose.

Certain now they were far enough away from their offices, Tierra stopped.

"What news are you hearing from outside," he asked Jee.

"It's a tangled mess everywhere," Jee reported.

"Say on," Tierra said.

"The recent exercises have thinned the field of workers, and created other associated hardships across the city," Jee said.

Tierra stifled a chuff at the reference to both the council's slaughter of Lelo's Orange Ring within the City and their attack on Louratna's mountain stronghold as *exercises*.

Tierra glanced up to Eldoro as the greater heat loomed above. "The black rot was already thinning the workers," he said.

"Yes. Several have died of that. But the exercises took several more, and fear of reprisal is stronger now."

Tierra twisted his lips.

He knew the truth of those words, just as he knew the other Families blamed him for these outcomes. He did not like being the *kashtan*—the blamed ones. It was true the Waganat Family had driven the decision, but *all* of them had joined.

Jee continued: "The city is growing tense. The transfer of so much of our stores to the Tegras has left us little to sell, and the few shops we have are not enough, and—across all Families—stores that do not open are being ... raided. I cannot think these tensions will remain unbroken for long."

Jee cast a sideways primary at Tierra. "Cash flow is becoming a problem."

"We are being looted."

"Yes, Master Waganat."

Tierra put both hands on the ball of his walking stick and let the report settle.

Since the *exercises* Tierra had already pressed much of his own workforce into salvaging inventory from several independent shops the Waganats were connected to—shops that now were either left ownerless or defenseless. Even in the best of times, security in the lower families' shops was always problematic, but now it was free season. Anything not locked down in their stores were subject to theft.

"Damned *hedgies*," he said.

"That's the surprising thing, Master Waganat. It is not the independent quadars doing damage to our business."

"What do you mean?"

"There are some who would prefer the Families see the lower families as delinquent."

"That's because they are."

"That is true enough as it goes. It is natural to *expect* the h*edgie* population would be first to scavenge because they *are* grimy, unhealthy, and of lesser foundation as quadars of the Families. Many of them no longer have the means to feed themselves so they have great need, and that need leads them to pretend it is somehow just to steal from us. But it's also true that this kind of expectation can be a cover for falsehood."

Jee paused.

Tierra did not reply, simply stood, contemplating as a gust of breeze blew up a dust devil in the distance.

"By that I mean such expectation makes a good cover story. The truth is more complicated, and therefore more useful to understand."

"I understood what you meant," Tierra snapped back. "So, what, in your opinion, is that truth?"

"*Hedgie* looters *do* come to pick the bones, but the activities that cause us the most damage are most likely being made by the Families—sometimes even dressed as *hedgie* invaders in order to further cover their tracks."

Tierra twirled the stick absently, letting his gaze take in a hut across the way.

It was a storehouse the Family used to stockpile its food.

At least they had defended that well enough.

His grip around the cane grew tight, then he tossed it upward to grab it by the throat. He looked at it, then. Fully contemplated it for the first time in a while.

The staff was smoothly polished, gleaming in the direct light of Eldoro's heat. Waganat branding had been seared into the shaft, the same Waganat branding that, in earlier days, when the Family was more devout in its Terilamat foundations, would certainly have been branded across his face or down his arms. The staff had been his father's and his grandfather's before that.

Tierra didn't need the cane to walk, but he liked carrying it because it felt like a weapon in his hand, heavy and strong.

He liked how the sway of its weight levered back and forth as he strolled.

He liked the sound it made as it struck the ground, that sharp crack that punctuated a moment.

It carried his father's aura, too.

Being so new to his position at the head of the Waganats, Tierra wasn't above taking any opportunity to remind lower quadars of who they were speaking with.

His primaries flashed to Jee, then back to the twisted path behind them, and, finally, to the city beyond.

"So, you're saying the Families are stealing from us?"

"That is what I am saying. They are taking steps to amass resources."

Tierra grimaced.

"If that is true…"

A cloud of desperation came over him. The smell of the ground, even now beginning to radiate heat as Eldoro climbed, seemed to encase him in a cloud of despair.

"Families hording resources is a clear sign of times to come."

"All the wiser for your arrangement with the Tegras."

Tierra accepted that for the compliment it was.

"What do you make of the Orange Ring?" he said.

"The Orange Ring?"

"Yes. What do you make of rumors surrounding whatever remains of Brada's rebels?"

Jee clicked his tongue. "They exist."

"But you think they cause no harm?"

"Without Lelo, they have no true leadership."

Tierra agreed with that. At one point he had assumed his brother would attempt to take his revenge on the Family by taking control of the Ring and accepting the identity of Lelo as homage to Brada, but that was a dumb idea to begin with. Baraq had never been one to *do* anything.

"What of the attack on the Tegra storehouse?" he said.

Jee shrugged. "What was taken? A few guns and a handful of crates."

"Was it the Ring?"

"Probably not. There are others, too."

"Others?"

"Revolution is nothing more than ignorant discontent, and there are many ignorant and discontented *hedgies* in Esgarat City now. I will compile a list of suspects later today if that will suffice. All anyone can say now is that these attacks do not seem to have been coordinated in any way, so I would not recommend spending resources on them if it were me."

Tierra nodded. "Fair assessment."

They walked back toward the offices in silence, then, watching Katon's lesser heat join Eldoro in the sky, Tierra stopped and turned his gaze to the workers toiling at the security wall. He shaded his central, feeling dry breeze against his face as he took in the double shadows that came from the sibling heats.

In a moment they would be back in the offices and their conversation would need to be guarded.

"I think we need to do two things, Jee," he finally said. "First we will need to go to the Council of Clans to discuss your accusations of the Families."

Jee gave a listless twitch of his shoulder. "Why? No one I speak with seems to think the council will matter."

Tierra waved his stick in a wide arc before them.

"You can see for yourself where we stand," Tierra said. "Everything needs to be rebuilt. We need more masonry and more stonework. We need even more hands. All of which are in short supply. Our repairs are well underway, but they are taking too long and you can only beat a *hedgie* to move so fast. We need the session now."

Jee El gave a grunt.

"We have guns now, though," Jee said. "And we have your agreement with the Tegra to provide connections to more labor in the future."

"Yes, but what we don't have is time."

Jee wrinkled his brow in confusion. "You will go to the council and arrange for more workers?"

"We have nothing left to bargain with," Tierra said, clicking a negative with a deeply annoyed sigh.

"Then, still. Why the council?"

"I want to keep them talking," Tierra said. "If what you say is true, then every Family in Esgarat City is preparing for war, but none have progressed on those preparations to the point they feel emboldened. Yet. The Council of Clans is fangless, but it *is* public. No Family will want to be blamed as the instigator. We can use that fear to prolong this sense of concern."

"I see," Jee said.

"We can't afford to lie to ourselves now, Jee. This is a dangerous period for that. If we are going to get those walls up, we need every moment we can get. Going to the council won't prevent the inevitable, but the Families' desires to make appearances should draw out the process."

"That is true," Jee said. "We could use more time."

"So," Tierra said, leveling his gaze at his assistant. "I need you to do two things."

"Anything I can do you know I'll do."

Tierra smiled at the sincerity on Jee El's face. "Yes, my friend, you've proven that many times over."

"What do you need?"

"First, I want a list of every Family that has taken material from any of our stores. That looting means a direct loss of income. There will come a time when the Waganat name is in power once again. We will remember them when that time comes."

"I will develop such a list."

"Excellent."

"And the second thing?"

Tierra scanned the field of debris, taking in the shattered ground before him and sensing his most personal of problems—the one he had to deal with now, or face the ramifications of further betrayal from inside the Family.

This devastation could not stand without response.

"By all accounts, my brother visited Louratna, but his body was not among those found among the mountainside dead."

"Perhaps he was simply lost in the count."

Tierra clutched his father's walking stick, feeling the truth of what that meant as he held the shaft so tight it hurt his hands.

"No," he replied with cold certainty. "To think that would be to believe in convenience, and I won't do that. I have no doubt Baraq is alive. Just as I have no doubt he will return to the city in some form."

"What is it you need, Master Waganat?"

Tierra cleared his throat and looked at Jee El.

"I need you," he finally said, "to find and kill my brother."

CHAPTER 10

The session had barely started when Brother Oast'el brought up his plan.

"All of our reports say that the Families are in precarious balance," he said. "We need to attack now."

They sat in the darkness at the open gap, faces touched by thin lighting that came from the flames of the three dim *taka* holders spaced out before them. The day's heat radiated from the stone they sat on. The proximity of body heat made the session both uncomfortable and intimate. Their first true planning session was always going to have been a nervous meeting, but now—from her position seated cross-legged in the circle—Ezi felt tension among the quadars so tight it crackled. Her skin tingled. A weight grew inside her chest.

Given Oast'el was now the ranking leader of what remained of the Orange Army, the words brought the session to a halt.

Ezi turned her exasperated gaze to him, sitting directly cross-circle, noting how his entire body spoke of rigidity and disagreement.

She had called the Ring together so it could begin to regroup, and work through plans for how to protect and feed the *hedgie* population, and to attempt to bring order to a world that was rapidly disintegrating.

The session was turning into something completely different.

A split had formed among the leadership ring now, some

wanting blood in return for their lost leader, others placing safety for their members above all other goals. Some, like her, wanted to focus on the longer game. Peace and prosperity, she thought, were only going to come with sacrifice.

"We have never been a violent group," she said. "I don't see why we should start now."

"Are you making jest of me?" Oast'el replied. "Did you not see what the Families did?"

Ezi glared, fighting an urge to rip skin off his face. "You truly believe we need to attack the Families right now?"

"You've heard the reports of vandalism in the city," he replied.

"I have."

"Someone is targeting the Families. They will blame us."

"Even if they do, I don't think direct retaliation is called for. If Brada were here, I can't imagine he would agree with confrontation now. It is not who we are."

"Brada's absence is what says we need to take different directions now. You say that we were not a violent group, and that was right, but true or not that is what the Families called us. You heard them."

"The quadars of Esgarat City knew better."

The fire crackled in the silence around them.

"Someone is coordinating aggressive acts, Ezi," Oast'el said after a moment to calm himself. "Even I can't bring myself to believe that a single quadar was able to destroy a Festia shop and infiltrate a Tegra storeroom all by themselves. It must be an organized approach. You expect the Families to see things differently?"

"It's possible," Ezi said, gazing around the circle. "They could all be isolated incidences."

"Sister Ezi." The voice came softly but directly.

"Yes, Sister Vareta," Ezi replied to the elder sister of the Ring.

Vareta gestured toward a nook of the inner cave where little Pella sat.

"This is no talk for a whelpling."

"Pella has been involved in our actions. She's earned the right to hear these conversations."

"I think that's unwise. We have already discussed questions a whelpling should be spared."

"I promise to be quiet," Pella said, her primaries suddenly

gleaming with the fear of being excluded.

"It's not about your silence, whelpling," Vareta said. "Young ears do not need to be cluttered with such things as the matters at hand. You will understand better as you get to your elder cycles."

"I agree," Oast'el said.

Others seemed to concur.

Ezi's hearts dropped as she saw a darkness pass Pella's face. The young quadar had already lost much through the early days of this skirmish. And while she was employed in the Waganat compound she'd been involved directly in their actions—both as a conduit to Baraq and as a part of the action that broke that Family's spine. The realization that the circle was going to remove her crossed her face as a dark cloud.

"I'm so sorry, Pella. I'll speak with you on this when we are finished."

"I won't leave," she said.

"Pella!" Ezi said with more force than she wanted.

There was a moment of quiet.

"I will speak with you about this when it is over."

The whelp's shoulders slumped. Defeated, she stood, then left.

"I'm sorry for that," Vareta said when Pella was gone. "It is for the better, though."

"Sister Pella deserves to be here as much as anyone," Ezi replied.

Vareta clucked a *we'll see* sound, then gestured for the group to move on.

"All right," Ezi said as she recentered herself. This session was too important to fight that battle now. "As I was saying, I think it's certainly possible that a single quadar with enough knowledge and time to plan could have achieved the results we hear of regarding the Festia and Tegra actions."

"The number of those walking Esgarat with that skill number few."

"But more than none," Ezi replied, her mind suddenly lighting up with questions. Who could it be? What member of the Orange Army might still be out there taking actions? Or would it be an independent *hedgie*?

Someone else?

"It makes no difference," Oast'el answered. "The Families will blame us. And we've seen what can happen when Family blood is raging. I don't care if you are Brada's pair-mate or not, the only way to address this is to go on the offensive."

Ezi slowly blinked her central.

She felt pressure build inside that matched what she felt from the circle. Her central narrowed hard enough the skin across her temples stretched. "Thank you for reminding us again that I was Brada's pair-mate," she said. "Sometimes I almost forget about that entirely."

"I am sorry, Ezi," Oast'el said. "I apologize for my bluntness."

She waved the comment off.

"I understand your view," she said. "In addition to having been Brada's pair-mate, I have also been in the circle for as long as there had been a circle. I have watched you and Brada wrestle with decisions on when to be aggressive and when not to be. I know your notions will always slant toward action."

"Perhaps if Brada—"

"Everyone here knows similar things can be said about your time with Brada, too, Oast'el," Ezi continued, forcefully cutting his conversation short. "We all know the story of how the two of you—despite your clan differences—became friends in the days when the Waganats sent their whelp to his schooling, and so, by that relationship alone, you are my friend, too. We also know you have fought both with and for Brada ever since, and that the Orange Army would not be in existence without you. By that relationship, you are a friend to all of us.

"An argument can be made that—while Brada was clearly the root of the whole of the Orange Ring—you and he were equally at the root of the revolution itself."

The gathering hung on Ezi's words.

Taka light flickered in Ezi's pause. The cave opening seemed to chill as they sat.

Pushing this had been a gamble, but it was a move she'd seen Brada use often. Rebuke, then grab control of a conversation and make a point about togetherness without direct attack. She'd been feeling the group swaying toward Oast'el's preferred approach. She'd needed to do something.

"As you, too, are at the root of the Orange Ring," Oast'el finally replied.

Ezi gave an internal sigh of relief.

She had trusted Oast'el to give her the opening, but his emotions were strained now. There had been no guarantee.

"We have both been in this for a long time," Ezi replied. "But none of that matters this heat."

"What is it you think matters then?" Oast'el said.

"Our numbers. More than anything. And the fact that we are crossing hard desert together. As we stand, our numbers are not large enough to waste even a single drop of energy. So what matters is that we come to a shared understanding of what we are doing, and then align the actions of our bodies such that every motion goes toward making that goal a reality. That shared understanding may well wind up being the direction you prefer, but my view is that I cannot see how direct conflict with the Families will work out well for us right now."

"We may be larger than you think," Sister Vareta said.

"In what way?"

"I don't think it's wise to completely discard the stories Oast'el refers to. We have goodwill in the city—or at least there are many who will consider us to be on their side. And lone vigilante or not, we clearly do have an ally in arms somewhere in the city."

"Or *allies* in arms," Oast'el added.

"And whether that *ally* was purposefully attempting to damage the Families or not," Vareta continued, "they have most certainly done damage, which is advantageous to us regardless of what directions we take. If nothing else, they have diverted the Families' attentions."

"This is where I make my argument," Oast'el said. "We need to push the Families now, while they are still scrambling."

The collective turned their gazes to Ezi.

She closed her triple eyes and let herself feel everything around her: The hard rock against her bottom and her legs, the harsh sensation of the wraparound over her shoulders and back, and the chill of the air against her plates. This was the moment. If the gathering chose to follow Oast'el now, the Orange Ring as she knew it—as Brada had grown it—was over.

Ezi collected herself, then opened her eyes, keeping her gaze focused on Oast'el.

"I miss him, too," she said.

"This is not about Brada," Oast'el said.

Ezi ignored him.

"We all do, I know. But I miss him differently.

"I feel him mostly late in the night.

"In those hours when I am alone and cannot sleep.

"When I cannot lay my arm over his softly rising chest to let the rhythm of his breathing take me back to my slumber.

"But I miss him here, too. I miss his ability to see truth and to focus our energies where they most need to be focused."

She paused and tried to feel as she would when Brada had spoken in these moments, tried to find a piece of the magic Brada could bring to the collective.

"I understand your desire for vengeance," she said. "And I'm not immune to it. I feel that need as deeply as you do. I *was* Brada's pair-mate. If there is a quadar in All of Esgarat who feels his loss more deeply than even you, Oast'el, it would have to be me, and though that does not give me any claim to the leadership of this gathering, it does give me this." She stopped. Her gaze crossed the room. "It gives me the ability to say that if Brada were here—if *Lelo* were here—he would say that he understands any quadar's desire for blood, but that we should not let our desire for vengeance cause us to do something rash. It is right to note the Families are in disarray, but they are still strong. And, while this news of renegade factions in the city is something we need to assess, we cannot afford additional losses now. It is right to mourn Brada. But it is also right to take into memory what happens when we address the Families head-on.

"Brada would see that.

"And he would find some miraculous way to bring this forward without creating offense. I am not Brada, though. My only tool is a direct statement. So, all I have to offer is this: That the idea of direct confrontation today is a bad idea. It will cost us dearly. There has to be a better way for us to save what's left of the lesser families and *hedgies* than to place ourselves into the direct line-sight of Family guns."

Ezi had been so focused on words coming from her mouth and the expression on Oast'el's face that she could not tell from which of the leaders came a click that suggested agreement.

Then came another. And another.

She waited for his response, watching as emotions crossed his face.

Oast'el moved a shoulder plate. "And what do you think is more important than cutting into the Families while we can?"

Another voice broke in. "Protecting the quadarti."

It was Vareta.

Attention turned to her.

"That is what Brada would have said," Vareta added. "We all know that in our hearts. Protect the quadarti. I agree with Sister Ezi. We are all hurting now. We are all distraught in our own ways over Brada's murder. But he would not want us to destroy what he built simply to avenge him. He would want us to make things better."

If Ezi could have, she would have reached over and kissed the elder quadar on the spot.

She suddenly felt so close to Brada she would swear she could feel his touch. The sensation was so intense she nearly collapsed, but his aura strengthened her and instead she sat up taller.

"My thanks to you, Vareta," Ezi replied, then turned to the rest of the collection—eleven quadars of various house affiliations and independences. "It's completely understandable to feel like Oast'el is feeling, but what Sister Vareta says is true. We have bloodied the Families, and the Waganats are now reeling. There will be a war among them for scraps."

"That war gives us opportunity," Oast'el said, making his last argument but leaving Ezi an opening she didn't miss.

"Yes, it does. But the opportunity it gives is to help as many free quadars as we can, and, in the process, help the Families weaken each other."

"I see an additional path," Vareta said.

Ezi gave a gentle motion of her central to indicate she go on.

"The foe of our enemy is possibly our friend," Vareta said. "I agree with Oast'el that we need to find out who these rebel quadars are and determine what they are doing. Are there things we could convince them to do that might heighten tensions between the Families?"

"Divert more attention away from *hedgie* families," Oast'el said.

Ezi looked to Oast'el. "I agree. It would be good to hear their stories. Do you think you can find them?"

"Thanks to Brada's earlier toils, we have many eyes in the city.

Should not be hard."

"Anything we can do without drawing direct attention would be perfect."

A gust of wind crossed the cave as the gathering sat in silence. Ezi felt a freshness as tensions faded.

"It's agreed, then?" Ezi said, glancing around the circle. "We'll help the vigilantes?"

Expressions around the circle told her this session had accomplished what it needed to accomplish. She was not Brada. No one was ever going to be Brada. But they had established a process by which they could make difficult decisions.

When no one dissented, Ezi moved on.

"All right then. What do we need to focus on to best help the quadars in Esgarat City?"

"Shelter and food," Vareta said. "Those are the first steps."

"Yes," came a reply from around the room.

"That seems the obvious answer," Vareta added. "Though it would likely mean parlaying with the Banit Family."

"Anyone can grow a plant," Oast'el said. "I do not like the idea of aligning with any Family."

Ezi had known that was coming. "I don't like aligning with any of the Families, either. Is it necessary?"

"It's not optimal," Vareta responded. "But we need more than a plant. The Banit Family controls agriculture throughout the lower hills. They know the cycles. They understand scale. I think it's either make a pact with them or set out more claims upslope, and that is not an option that helps anyone today."

"We can learn to harvest."

"Eventually, yes."

The ring sat in silence, understanding the unspoken part.

"Do either of you have better ideas?" Vareta asked.

"No," Ezi said. "I don't."

Oast'el clicked a negative.

"It is agreed then?" Vareta said.

The group conferred.

Ezi took a deep breath, then released it. The Orange Ring had come around even more robustly than she'd imagined.

She felt lighter already.

OF THE FITTEST

CHAPTER 11

The morning Torrance and Crissandr planned to set off for Esgarat City, Torrance woke from his dreams too early.

He realized he'd been dreaming because, though he couldn't recall details, his mind was buzzing with that unsettling mix of joy and anxiety that made him feel like he was on nettles as he lay on his pallet. He knew it was too early because the only light in his chamber was that of the dim luminescence that came from the moss-covered rock he'd placed on the stand across the room.

Having learned cave patterns well enough now, he could travel through most of those passages in the total darkness. He didn't need the moss's light, but it made him feel better, made him feel safer and somehow more at home. A decanter of water stood on the stand, too, and an almost ripe *dashtar* fruit beside that, waiting for him to break his fast when the proper time came.

He lay still, absently noting the luminescence of the moss-covered rock while trying to reclaim sleep.

The pallet pressed into his shoulder and hip. His legs throbbed with the dull ache of too much use over the past several days. He would like to blame his restlessness on that, but he knew it was something else.

Launch day had always been like this, too.

In truth he didn't like to travel.

The thought almost made him chuckle. Here he was, Torrance Black, a kid from Wisconsin, waking up in a cave on a distant planet encircling Alpha Centauri A, and he was feeling *travel anxiety* about a trip around some mountains.

He opened his eyes fully but, as if still thinking he could make his way back to sleep, did not give in to temptation to move.

Per quadar norm, he'd positioned the pallet in the middle of his chamber, which was an alcove Louratna had first assigned him—specifically because it was near the surface and his eyes would benefit from the small crevasse that allowed natural light to filter in.

Given his position and closeness with Louratna, the quadars here had told him to take her chambers now, which were deeper in the cave and hence viewed as preferable to them. He hadn't been able to do that, though. Those walls felt too much like her for him to be comfortable in them. So instead, he had stayed here, where he'd been since he arrived—an alcove carved by water millennia ago—water that still existed on this planet but had retreated downward into the depths of the caves.

As he lay still on his side, Torrance saw that only starlight touched the rough contours of that crevasse, hence confirming his assessment of the time.

If that stone had not been dark, though, the chill alone would have been enough for Torrance to call it nighttime. This mountainside faced direct light from both Eldoro and Katon, and he'd been here long enough that he could sense how the chamber's thermal profile had changed over the cycles—it was cool in the mornings but was now often too warm after the pair of suns had risen for any time at all.

Torrance didn't like being too negative, but the pattern matched so many others. Regardless, the thermal gradients made for another form of analog clock he'd been learning how to read.

Despite the hour, his thoughts raced.

There was a lot to do.

Finally giving up, Torrance breathed a waking breath and rolled onto his back, allowing himself free range to think about the day ahead and feeling the acidic churn of anxiety that was balling up in his stomach.

"You are awake."

The quadarti voice in the darkness startled him, but only for a moment. He rolled to his other side.

"Crissandr," he said, rolling up and feeling the stretch of his legs and back as he sat cross-legged before her.

In the dim light he saw her form seated against the far chamber wall, her legs drawn up, lanky arms wrapped around them such that her fingers cupped her knees. She wore a *haldi* he was familiar with, drapes of its hem now spilling over the stone floor. Dark shadow bathed her primaries, but her central flared with a golden radiance when the moss light struck at the proper angle.

"I did not wish to wake you," she replied.

"It's fine. I couldn't sleep anyway." The language was beginning to come more easily between them, he thought as he stretched and came more fully awake. He'd been spending more time with Crissandr since they returned from the desert and began to plan their travels.

"Much to think about," she said.

"*Chah*," Torrance clicked as best he could to reply in the affirmative. "Much to do."

Their travel to Esgarat City would take him away from the mountains for some time. To make a good faith offer to Baraq meant his first goal was to ensure the rocketry production facilities were at least partially operational when he returned.

Edart Kel would be in charge.

She was exceptionally good—having been instrumental in designing and producing the fueling system that allowed their first successful launch—but she was also awkwardly young. He wanted to go over everything with her one more time—check on the status of plans for clearing the floor of debris, then prioritize the list of machines and stations that she needed to repair first. Fuel development was also premium. They wouldn't be ready for fueling for weeks but creating the volume they were going to need was a long-pull item. It had to be ready when the time came.

Casting ovens were next.

Assembly and testing stations.

His mind spun out of control.

And that was all before he even got to the tasks of checking through the items they would need for their trip.

Shelter.

Supplies and foodstuffs.

Crissandr would do all that, too, but he wouldn't be happy until he had put eyeballs on it all.

At least the Families had left behind a derelict motor cart. It had been nothing but junk to them, but young Jatara—who was so good with mechanics that Torrance suggested Edart take her as an apprentice—had found a way to get it working again.

He didn't think it would withstand a rugged mountain expedition, but he'd been wrong before and, even if it failed at some point, it would save wear and tear on his still-aching legs.

"It will be a difficult trip," Crissandr said, breaking into his thoughts. "I do not know if I will return."

"Me, too."

It was the first time he'd vocalized that fear.

He was getting old, nearing eighty standards as best as he could tell. With proper care and life extension technologies available in the Solar System he could live another fifty or eighty years. But Esgarat was not the Solar System. His body was wearing out quickly. He felt every knock and cut now in ways he never had before.

And the terrain was going to be harsh.

The trip *could* kill him.

"Perhaps you should stay here," Crissandr said.

"What?"

"I do not want you *indati*," she said, stressing the quadarti word. "You should stay."

"I'm not leaving you to go alone. This was my idea to begin with."

"They need you here, Torranze. Without you, we cannot remake your rockets."

"The rockets won't be enough if we don't have anyone to make them. We need more workers to help. And we need—"

"I can carry your words to him."

Torrance shook his head, feeling the hole that lay behind Crissandr's avoidance of Baraq's name.

Over the past few heats Torrance had shared his plans with Crissandr, so what she was proposing was technically feasible. She could carry his offer to Baraq. But that wouldn't be good enough. Baraq had been an inventor in his past. He was an engineer at heart. It was Baraq himself who had managed the first investigations into the wormhole pod Torrance had sent here in the first place. Torrance needed his expertise.

It went deeper than that, too. Deeper than simple logistics or project management.

They needed to trust each other.

They needed to be of the same mindset, so they needed to spend time in the same place at the same time.

"You can carry my offers, but you cannot carry how I think," Torrance said. "Without Baraq we are on our own. I need to speak with him."

When Crissandr sat in silence for long enough, Torrance leaned forward, his expression asking the question he wanted asked.

"Baraq has changed," she said.

"Changed?"

Her chest heaved with a large breath, which he heard exhaled in the darkness of the cave.

"The Families killed our whelpling, Torranze. And they've already tried to kill Baraq himself once and failed."

"I know that," Torrance said. "And with due respect it wasn't the Families that tried to kill him. It was the Waganats."

"Do not speak of what you don't understand."

"I do understand."

"No. You do not."

"I understand Baraq cares for his people. His quadars."

"He did. Yes. At one time he was open and wise. He had a picture of the future then. A dream." A breeze over the gap in Torrance's chamber resonated with a gentle whistle. The tone of Crissandr's voice seemed intimate in the near darkness. Torrance saw pain etched in her posture.

"And now?"

The whistling died, and Torrance could hear Crissandr's breathing. Her fingers gripped harder on her knees, as her gaze went to the gap in the ceiling.

"The Families killed more than our child."

"I see."

Crissandr chuffed in the darkness and suddenly Torrance saw something he hadn't before.

"You want to save him," Torrance said.

She clicked a soft neutral. "I miss him."

Crissandr was pragmatic to the bone—a person who did what

must be done. But despite all her pragmatism she had lost so much. Her only daughter cycles before, and her only son at the hands of the Family she had married into.

Now this.

He understood parts of the story.

When Baraq had left the mountain, it was not only Baraq who had chosen to leave Crissandr. She had turned away from him, too. She had told him she would not go back to Esgarat City with him, though that is what he asked of her. At first Torrance had seen that decision in a simple frame, but now all the pragmatic explanations in the universe couldn't cover the fact that hers was a complex situation in a complex world.

Baraq—who had once pursued the Taranth Stone with a purpose borne of curiosity and love for his people—did what he did now out of anger and a quest for vengeance that Crissandr could not bring herself to, yet he was all she had left.

It was true, he thought. In destroying Lelo, the Families had taken more from her than a son.

Now Torrance himself was about to offer Baraq tools that might well feed whatever desperation had now filled her pair-mate's mind but could also potentially help save him.

"You think I don't understand," Torrance finally said.

"I know you don't understand." Her voice was thick in the darkness.

"Well," Torrance replied. "You might be right. But I'm not leaving you to travel alone."

As they sat in silence, the rays of Eldoro rising began to touch the crevasse rock. Crissandr stood, then ran her hand down the front of her loose *haldi*, her expression resigned.

"It was worth an attempt."

A moment later, she left.

CHAPTER 12

Torrance spent the first half of the morning letting Edart Kel guide him through her preparations. The cavern was big and echoed with the activity of the cleanup. He enjoyed being with the young quadar.

He felt closer to her now, too.

Beyond the obvious aspects of their natural curiosities and their propensities for invention, the sense of shared experience bonded them now, too. Edart was the quadar who had guided him out of the caves during the Families' raid, and therefore saved his life. She had been shot in the skirmish, too, but recovered well enough by now that her limp was nearly gone. Or, at least, her passion for the work overrode any problems her leg might be causing her.

Despite the situation, she was vibrant and excitable. It was hard not to smile at her energy.

She reminded him of young Thomas Kitchell when he was a whelpling. She was as daring as Kitchell had been, although not as carefree. He could not, for example, imagine the phrase *hey, take a chance* coming from her lips with such flippancy as Kitchell had pulled off.

But, like Torrance had experienced with Kitchell, they had been through a war together. That Edart had quickly picked up the mishmash of qualish he and Louratna had grown between them made it even easier to like her.

"*Mata,*" he said after she finished her tour. "It's all looking very good."

The Families had destroyed the cavernous area the rocket program had been using as a production line. Until the last heat or two, the area had been in total disarray, but Edart and two other quadars had done some creative thinking and developed a motorized cart and pulley system to carry debris away. He could suddenly envision the work finishing quickly now.

"I expected the cleanup would take many days," Torrance said. "There's still a lot of work to do, but you're way ahead of schedule."

Edart beamed. "I want to be building rockets before you return, Torranze."

He couldn't help but smile at the quadars' pronunciation of his name. The quadarti tongue wasn't as practiced at the soft "c" as a human's was, but he found he liked the buzzy way the name felt when Edart or the rest of the community said it.

"I hope I'm not gone that long," he said.

"I hope we are that fast," Edart replied.

Torrance nodded, then put his hand on her shoulder to draw her attention.

"I want you to do something more, Edart," he said.

"What is it?"

He sighed, knowing he was about to ask her to change the entire focus of the effort and knowing that this change might affect her in ways that were both predictable and not. "We need to make the rocket's body smaller."

"Smaller?"

He held his hands together, fingertip to fingertip, making a circle with his fingers and thumbs. "Yes, about this size. Maybe a little smaller. I need you to design it that way."

She matched his gesture. "How do we load the aerosols?"

"I'll say more about that later. But now I also want tubes smelted and cast. Make them the length of your arm, give or take. Same size around as the rocket—just big enough that the rocket fits into them."

Edart's lips twitched as she thought.

The skin over Edart's cheekbones darkened.

"I see," she said. "You want to make a gun."

Torrance felt his cheeks growing red. He should have known Edart would grasp the meaning of these changes immediately.

"How do you feel about that?"

Edart contemplated the question. She raised a six-fingered hand to scratch at the back of her neck as noises from the facility washed over them.

The sounds seemed to grow in volume, rock scraping against rock, metallic echoes of debris falling into wheelbarrows, the voices of the quadarti workers as they bent to the task. The grind of a conveyor belt kicked on.

Through it all, the fingertips on Edart's opposite side brushed absently at the place of her leg where a Family bullet had pierced it.

Watching her, an overwhelming sense of being came over Torrance. Until this moment, his anger had been about vengeance. Until now, he had fallen back on the image of a Family official executing Louratna and the cold, vacant hole that filled his chest whenever he thought of her.

Now, as Torrance watched young Edart come to this harsh understanding of reality, a new sense of resolve built inside him.

Edart was the future.

She represented everything Louratna cared about.

"I came here to be away from everything about Esgarat City," she replied. "I came to be part of something special. But that seems impossible now."

She paused there, as if looking for additional words.

Nothing further came though.

Instead, she gave the subtle tick of her arm that was the quadarti form of a shrug.

Torrance opened his arms wide.

Edart took a step into his hug and as his arms enclosed her, he felt her thin arms wrap around his own body, felt each of her thin fingers of both hands pressed individually against his back. They stood there for a moment that Torrance realized would never leave him, that he would remember that feeling forever, six fingers, thin and firm as a brand on each of his shoulder blades, the pressure of her forehead on his shoulder. The sensation made him happy. It made him feel like the world was here for a reason.

"I'm sorry," he whispered. "I wish it wasn't this way."

"Me also."

She stepped back, already resolved.

"I know you have to leave now," she said. "Travel well. I'll have things ready by the time you return."

CHAPTER 13

Eldoro had barely peered over the horizon when Karshi Fael saw movement at the mouth of the caves.

As was her practice, she was sitting on a flat rock in the ritual she used to welcome the coming heat, chewing on *katja* root between moments of thanking each of the elements of the land for their purpose. She sat there, feeling connected to her home as the whole of that land adjusted to the appearance of the heats—*pax* rodents scampering for safety as the *jah* took wing, flowering plants closing into thick pods. *Piela* lizards and other soft-bellied creatures emerging to lay on the stones to soak up heat.

There were so many fewer now than before. So many fewer.

The wild *katja* she'd pulled on her overnight scavenging rounds was light and sweet in the way she liked best, but also came with a bittersweet tinge that she felt to her bones. *Katja* was becoming a dying breed on the heat-side of the range. Few such plants survived darktime scavengers now. Already there was no *old katja* root. She felt a truth in the movements around her and in the taste of that *katja*. Time was coming when the surface slopes wouldn't support her anymore. Time was coming when she would have to leave.

Which was annoying.

She liked the mountains. She liked the music the wind made as it whistled over the peaks, liked the quickening pulse she felt while watching packs of *neantha* on the hunt, and she enjoyed the depth of the sensation she still got while watching a majestic *jah* soar upward on hot updrafts.

There was an essential beauty to the mountainside she couldn't find anywhere else.

It made her feel alive—even those moments she spent with her shoulder plates pressed against the cool, shaded side of rocks simply to avoid having her blood turn to mud inside her veins. The mountains gave her a connection to these grounds.

But facts were facts, and Karshi Fael had long ago realized that neither the desert nor the mountain would spare those who pretended otherwise.

If food no longer grew in the ranges, she would have to move on—either retreat deeper into the caves or set out to the vast realms where true free-rangers found ways to keep themselves alive despite all suggestions that it should be otherwise.

Maybe go west to Harshish Point where the *katja* fields were plentiful or east into the wild flatlands.

Or east to Extico.

She thought, for a moment, of Gar'et who—assuming he still lived—would be in Extico, and who would always be happy to welcome her back.

She was surprised at the way that idea made her feel.

She was getting older.

Maybe it was time to find a place to stay.

Those were the thoughts she set aside when her central noticed the motion in the caves.

Two figures emerged from the shadows that led from the chasm that Louratna's quadars used as primary egress.

The first was Crissandr, a quadar Karshi recognized as having been an active member of Louratna's community for many heats and as being a pair-mate to the one known as Baraq Waganat. Karshi had never spoken with Baraq Waganat, but knew the Family was a dangerous one, and knew he had been at the Council of Clans on the day she had dragged the near-dead foreign creature she had found in the deserts into their halls.

She ground her teeth together when she realized the other being that emerged from the chasm *was* that foreign creature.

The one who had fallen from the sky in a ball of flame, and who she had personally retrieved from the harsh desert cycles prior, dragging him over the ground for heats in hopes the Families could tell her what its appearance meant. Torranze, quadars in Louratna's family called him. The one Louratna's clan had stolen away with, and the one who had helped Louratna's community to craft the fire rocks they launched into the sky.

Torranze had caused Louratna's death by bringing worry to the Families.

Such was life in All of Esgarat.

Everything was action and consequence.

She knew only a small amount about how Family control worked in Esgarat City, but what she knew was more than enough to make her aware that bringing Family ire was a sure way toward an early return to the mountain.

It was that aspect of the Families that meant she could never live in their community.

Just the idea made her curl up inside.

So much better to live a life of the mountains, as true quadars were born to do.

Intrigued, though, Karshi watched the pair exit the cavern and move to the center of the clearing—to the same place where, heats before, Louratna's dead body had fallen. Torranze guided a motor cart of some form beside him. Crissandr held wrapped packages. Stores, Karshi though. Food and material they would need to travel. When they made it fully into the clearing, Crissandr placed the packages into a side cart, and the two of them took positions on the machine's seat, which was a long board spanning front to back, carved to make room for legs.

A moment later the blatting noise of an engine broke the morning calm, disturbing a chattering flock of tiny *dinka* strongly enough that they took wing into the coming heat.

The two left then, heading eastward down the slope.

Karshi's gaze followed their path. Esgarat City, she thought. That's where they would head. She knew the paths—looping and rugged. It was the direction Baraq had gone on foot, so much earlier. It was where, obviously, the Families had come from and then gone back to after destroying so much of Louratna's compound.

The aroma of the cart's exhaust came to her even from there, affixing the memory of Louratna's death that much more firmly into her mind.

If she closed her eyes and tried, Karshi could still feel that day.

The sound of the gun's explosion.

Louratna's body falling.

Karshi swallowed the last of the *katja* and spread her hands over the rugged rock she sat on.

Eldoro's heat was already touching the coarse surface.

Katon would be up soon, too, and then the heat would once again begin to twist in her vision of the horizon, coming as waves in a blast furnace, stretching the curve of the ground against the sky.

She gazed west, toward Harshish Point, thinking about the free-range quadars who lived there.

How long did they have before the Families would come for them, too? Or before the heats would burn the life from their lands? What would happen to them over the cycles? She didn't know the answers to any of these questions, but she did know that whatever those answers were, free-range quadars would have a response. And that at least she could live life there as she would want to.

Harshish Point, then, she decided. That was where she would go.

Not yet of course.

The trip there would be hard, so she would need to gather more food and spend time in the caves filling her body with water. She wiggled her toes, feeling rock under the thinness of her sandal soles. It would be good to mend them, too.

Her father had instilled that discipline in her as a whelpling.

Happy feet, happy Karshi, he had said to her back then.

It was, she considered, the most important idea he'd left her with.

CHAPTER 14

Wind tousled what little hair Torrance still had as he sat behind Crissandr. Hard stone and bramble rolled past under the cart's fiber tires. Time had flown by as easily as the landscape. After an initial sense of adventure, the sound of the motor grinding away made a great backdrop for daydreaming.

He'd been playing conversations in his mind—thinking about what he would say to Baraq—when the cart bounced hard on a depression in the rock, rousing Torrance from the reverie his brain had wandered off to.

He tightened his grip around Crissandr's waist and scanned the landscape around them again.

The engine's bleating was enough to scare away any natural predator for kilometers around, but it wasn't natural predators he was worried about. He'd been on the lookout for sentries the Families might have left behind, but the trip had been clean and easy so far. Unlike on Earth or several other planets he'd been on that had more habitable environments, vegetation here was thick up in the mountains where temperatures tended to be lower. Now that they were descending toward the floor, there were fewer places for sentries to stay hidden.

He felt relieved.

The motor cart—a three-wheeler that felt to Torrance more like a motorcycle than a car—gave a ragged sputter as it carried them through the foothills where the slope wasn't as steep as before.

Crissandr had taken the first shift simply because she was the one more familiar with the rugged ground in the upper regions of the mountain.

It was going to be a long trip, though.

His turn to drive was coming soon.

Like most vehicles he'd seen on the planet, the motor cart ran on a coarse and unpredictable mixture of kerosene and nitric acid that the quadars mined out of mountain ores. Even with the extra skin of fuel they were carrying with them, he didn't think the cart would get them the whole way to Esgarat City, but they could stash it after they ran out, and come back for it later. As they descended, the aroma of its exhaust mixed with arid air to sharpen his senses.

Truth was, he had no idea how long the fuel would last—but at least this batch was good enough to fire the engine. He'd seen cases where it wasn't strong enough.

Riding in the back, feeling the heat of Eldoro burning the skin at his neck, Torrance considered the idea of using solar power. It would work—as a direct power source, anyway. He'd seen some carts configured that way, but as far as he could tell, quadars had limited battery tech. They were all short-range vehicles with a spare, few minutes range at best. But on a planet with such bountiful sunlight, that would be less of an issue than on others.

He kicked himself for not thinking harder on it earlier.

He'd been so focused on the rockets, though, and no solar power in the world would get a rocket to escape velocity from a sitting start.

That was his excuse, anyway.

Crissandr guided them onto a flat slope.

Majestic, sheer cliffs of bright orange rock rose to their left. Harsh plains of broiling desert lay off to the right, plains that rolled away to almost melt into the distant horizon. He admired the tangled foliage the grew above the tree line, and the harsh plant life that clung to the rock here. He considered *pax* and *jah* and *razo* and *rela* and the hundreds of other animals, bugs, and flora that he remembered seeing in the open desert. Esgarat—Eden—was a harsh land, but a beautiful one, a land where life fought hard every day simply to exist.

But it did exist.

For an instant he recalled an image of a waterfall that had been on a wall during a long-ago meeting he'd taken in Captain Romanov's quarters.

He laughed then.

Wind whipped his hair, and Crissandr—who had apparently been feeling her own sense of freedom—bent over the guiding yoke.

She pressed the throttle, and the cart jumped ahead faster.

"You're a daredevil!" he screamed over the engine's whine.

Crissandr gave her own joyful cry back at him and they both lived the moment of speed as their cart rolled downhill and approached an area that would wrap around the cliff ahead.

"Hold on, Torranze!" she yelled as she pressed the throttle.

The engine coughed, and the tires whined against stone.

He grabbed her tight.

Crissandr couldn't have described the physics of centers of gravity or moment arms in any way, but she instinctively slowed a touch as they entered the curve. Both leaned into the turn just enough that their little motor cart stayed upright, but not enough to cut the thrill of being on the edge.

Torrance's heart pounded with something he thought might be glee.

She guided the cart into the apex of her curve, approaching nearer the rocky cliff face as she turned.

The surface flashed by in a blur.

He was so near the cliff now he thought he could reach out and touch it.

Torrance gave a big whoop. He hadn't felt this free since ... well ... since farther back than he could remember.

Crissandr let out a sudden yelp and yanked the yoke hard right.

Torrance whipped his head around fast enough to see forms ahead.

Huge figures.

Dark brown.

Tal beasts!

Torrance recognized them in a flash. A pack of wild *tal* beasts were on the shade side of the pass, grazing on vines that grew between cracks in the cliff.

Crissandr and Torrance's approach caused them to scamper, their thick bodies thundering away as they scattered in random directions.

The motor cart hooked hard right, then a wheel caught a rut, and it jerked the other way.

Torrance found himself airborne, screaming.

The ground rushed at him.

Humpfh.

He rolled hard over his shoulder and tumbled against the rough ground. Crissandr's scream mixed with the crashing sound of the machine tumbling, the growl of the engine, and the sirens of the *tal* in full retreat.

Torrance came to a stop, and the engine died with a single caustic cough.

He gulped air.

Sensations of pain began to seep in from his elbows, knees, and shoulder.

"Crissandr?" Torrance called.

She gave a moan from somewhere he couldn't place.

With a grunt, Torrance lifted himself up against his pain.

Crissandr lay in a heap against the cliff face. Red-brown blood was rolling down one side of her face.

The motor cart was a mangled mess lying on its side a distance down the road.

But what caught Torrance's eye was a single massive *tal* beast that had turned back toward them, head lowered to show the hard, bony pad at the top of its head. The animal made a guttural sound from deep inside its body and steadied itself, focused directly on Crissandr.

"Hey!" he called, scrambling to his feet despite a knee he thought was going to give out.

The beast was going to charge her.

"No!" he screamed, ignoring pain as he rushed to fill the space between them.

Approaching the upended vehicle's side cart, Torrance grabbed the sack of food Crissandr had prepared. Whirling it over his head like a sling, Torrance ran toward the *tal.*

The animal took a step toward Crissandr, but in a final lunge that toppled him back to the ground, Torrance brought the sack down on its head.

The beast halted, then reared on its haunches.

Torrance smelled the thing then, a thick musk clotting the back of his throat.

Saw its red-lined eyes.

Heard the clack of its broad, flat teeth as they ground together.

Frozen in fear, he watched as the *tal* beast's immense hooves raised up high in the sky over him.

This is it, he thought. *This is how it ends.*

Instead, the beast came down with a monstrous thud, then turned and ran off—sauntering a few paces down the lane after realizing Torrance wasn't following it.

Torrance stood again, panting, gripping the bag so hard his hands hurt.

The *tal* left.

Once convinced the animal was leaving, Torrance lowered the bag and went to Crissandr.

She lay on her side, propped up on one arm, the other hand over the brow of her eye where blood still welled.

"*Mata?*" he said, unable to get more out than the qualish word for *good*. Are you good? He hoped that's what she'd heard.

"Yes. Yes. *Mata.*"

She did not look *mata*.

Her *haldi*, which moments ago had been fluttering in the breezes caused by speed, was now tattered and torn in several places. Her skin had abrasions that were now also beginning to well blood. Nothing appeared broken, but she held one leg at an odd angle.

Torrance pulled his shirt up over his head and pressed a handful of its cloth against her bloody brow.

Crissandr tried to stand but didn't make it.

She gave a groan that Torrance took as an admonition, and she moved his hand from her head.

"Don't sit up if it hurts," Torrance said.

"*Mata!*" Crissandr called.

After she arranged herself to be sitting upright at the base of the cliff, she at least let him apply pressure.

She mumbled to herself, obviously angry.

It took a few moments, but the blood flow stanched. She stood successfully then, testing her leg with an understated grumble. She could stand, and she could hobble, but both ankle and knee were worse for wear and tear.

Did quadarti physiology include sprains and such?

Would she stiffen up with time?

He didn't know, but he couldn't see why not.

"Are you going to be able to walk?"

"Only know if we try."

Torrance took her opposite side elbow and helped her limp back to the motor cart. The crash had bent the steering yoke in half, and two of the three wheels were now out of line. The tire on the one good wheel had been shredded against sharp rock.

It wasn't going anywhere any time soon.

"Where is Jatara when you need her?" Crissandr said.

Torrance wasn't focused on the wreckage, though.

His attention went to a pair of hooks that had held their water sacks.

One dangled in midair, still full.

The other was gone.

He turned back down the path to see the busted skin lying on the path behind, the dark stain of its liquid making a trail that flowed in forked streams down the mountain slope.

Crissandr's expression said that she too understood their plight.

"Long walk," she finally said, reaching down to grab the full skin. "Might as well get on with it."

"All right," Torrance replied. He didn't think they could make it, now. But the only alternative was to simply give up.

He tied his bloody shirt around his neck and over his shoulders, then picked up the pack he had hit the beast with.

They would have food at least.

Returning to Crissandr's side, he took her elbow.

The two of them made their way farther down the mountain.

CHAPTER 15

"Hold that side right there," Edart Kel yelled over the loud screams of a grinding motor. "Firmly!"

She pressed herself against a lever on her side of the belt, straining.

On the opposite side of the conveyor system, Zvin Tek—a cohort she'd assigned to this task due to his strength and stamina over his brains—took a deep breath, then braced himself against the lever that held an axle in place.

Edart steeled every muscle in her body, which—though enough light filtered into the cavern now that she was already keeping her central closed—included clenching her primaries shut and grinding her jaw muscles against the strain. Bending harder to the task, and with one final burst of energy, the pair of them ratcheted the top belt tighter.

She stood taller and blinked sweat from her primaries as it oozed from her brow glands.

The belt connecting two pulley devices was taunt across its span.

"It's working!" Zvin said as he panted with exertion and watched as smaller bits of refuse on the upper belt fell into the lower tray across the distance.

Both trays traveled on toward the opening that led to the surface.

"You don't have to sound so surprised," Edart replied.

"I'm sorry," Zvin said too quickly, blanching despite himself, clearly taken aback.

Edart giggled but was immediately sorry. "Don't worry, Zvin," she said. "I'm just having fun."

The young quadar did not seem relieved.

Zvin wasn't the most opaque quadar in the compound, which meant she'd known he had interest in her some time ago, something that had become even more obvious once she'd chosen him for this assignment and he'd begun throwing himself into every directive she'd given him.

If she were being honest, she didn't mind the attention.

And if she were being *completely* honest, Zvin Tek was more than attractive. Seeing him standing there, chest heaving, muscles bulging with lifeblood, every part of his stance proclaiming he was also proud of his work, made her happy in ways she was certain she didn't want to reveal. She was of the Hlrat clan. He was Kandar. Though neither of them seemed to be actively practicing traditions, and though here in Louratna's community a quadar's clan of origin shouldn't matter, somehow it suddenly did.

It was midheat.

Despite its size, the rocket production cavern was hot, the air stagnant and full of sharp rock dust that clogged her nose like thick paste. It was dry and bitter when she swallowed. Her body was shedding liquid so quickly that her work shirt stuck to her skin and made her feel grimy. The cavern's echoey walls amplified the conveyor system's motor to a level so loud it hurt.

The work to clear out the production facility had been harder than she had initially planned.

The conveyor device certainly helped—and it would be even better if this gravity feed runner worked to properly separate smaller debris from larger as she designed it to. But the hardest part was still gathering the debris to begin with. The Families' attack had left her with only ten production workers, and, of those, three were still injured to the extent that it slowed their efforts. There was only so much bending and shoveling a quadar could do before needing rest.

It was clear now that simply clearing the production floor would take several more heats.

No reason to stop, though, Edart thought as she gazed at the rubble flowing over the belt. She fully expected to keep her promise to Torranze, and every little bit brought her that much closer to hitting that goal.

Together, she and Zvin watched the conveyer take material that others dumped on it out of the facility.

Once removed, the larger rocks—some she would even call small boulders—would simply be released to tumble down the mountainside. Smaller bits of detritus would form mounds that quadars could sift through manually to determine if the heap held salvageable metals. At that point, being certain that the remaining rubble was simply that—rubble—another machine would grind the finer bits into the pasty, mudbrick material they would use to build better defenses.

"It seems like we might break a few less belts if we put a support rod halfway down," Zvin said.

Edart looked to the span Zvin pointed to.

"I think you're right," she replied, eyes narrowing.

"You don't have to sound so surprised."

She laughed then. "I'm sorry again, Zvin. That was unfair."

He appeared to relax now.

The conveyor motor, no longer under maximum stress, settled into a lower hum.

Zvin stepped deftly around the engine to stand beside her. His expression drew down into a darker frame. "I wanted to ask you a question while I could," he said, speaking in a lower tone due to their proximity.

"You always can."

He ignored that comment, glancing first up to the flues that gave the chamber its ventilation, then back to the conveyor before settling on the ground between them.

"What is it?" Edart asked.

"What do you think is going to happen to us now?"

Edart gave him a questioning glance.

"It's not just me," he said. "All of the workers are wondering. There are stories that the Families are going to return to finish their work. And if that doesn't happen, there is still a question of how we proceed without Louratna. You are close with Torranze. We know he matters. What do you think is going to happen to us now?"

"That's not a question I like to think about. Better to just stay busy. Focus on the problems at hand and make things better."

"There is much talk of leaving for the desert."

"Well," Edart said. "I think that's a bad idea."

"What is here for us if we remain?"

Edart stared into Zvin's gaze and saw a root of desperation she couldn't bring herself to avoid.

His question was valid.

What *was* on the other side of this?

And as Zvin stood there with his expression of anticipation, Edart felt a new emotion cross her mind: Louratna was dead, Torranze and Crissandr were gone. Louratna had other quadars who she sought occasional council with, but without either Louratna, Crissandr, or Torranze here, the community under the mountain was looking to her for their leadership.

She *was* the rocket program now, and the rocket program was now the entire reason this place existed.

It was suddenly hard to breathe.

She gathered herself, but still the idea prickled her skin.

"It's a hard question to answer," she finally replied.

"We came here to be who we are," Zvin replied. "All of us—*hedgie* or not. We came here to learn. We came for the work and for the sense of freedom that comes from being out from under Family grip. If you are like me, the idea of going back to Esgarat City is like death—but the Families have shown us that to stay here could be no different."

He paused for a breath. "So, what else is there, Edart Kel? You say that going to the desert is a bad idea, but what do we have left for us here?"

He waited, feet planted.

She gave a movement of her hands and shoulders.

"I don't know," she finally replied.

She looked up at Zvin then, looked at him in ways she hadn't looked at him before. She peered past the fear she had seen a moment before, saw his attraction for her. She looked beyond all that, and beyond his youthful anxieties and his awkward sense of self, she saw an essence of nobility. Zvin Tek worked hard because he liked it, and because it was the right thing to do. And she saw something more, too. The rest of the background behind this conversation.

Zvin was speaking for the workers—workers who had also seen his nobility, though they would not have said this aloud. Instead, they had shown their respect for him by asking him to talk to her, and he had done so despite all those barriers she had just seen beyond.

"I *am* like you," Edart finally said, putting her hand on his elbow. "I cannot stomach the idea of returning to Esgarat City either. I believed in Louratna, too. She was why I came here. And I can't say I know what future heats will bring from the Families better than anyone else. But if anyone says they do know the answers to those questions, I suggest closing your primaries to them."

"Would you ever leave for the desert?"

"Maybe someheat. But it is too early for that in my mind. None of the ideas Louratna held dear have changed. If anything, her execution makes her positions even more firm."

"You still think we can save All of Esgarat."

"Yes," Edart said, surprising herself with the strength the word had as she said it.

Zvin gave an exasperated sigh and scanned the husked-out shell of the room that stood before them.

"I believe we can do it," she replied, still with too much bluster. "There are problems, of course," she said, calming herself with her own words. "Lots and lots of problems—as there will always be. I believe in Torranze, though. He consulted with Louratna. They arrived at their plans together, and he knows what he is doing. He helped us build this all the first time. I have to believe he can do it again."

"With your help," Zvin said, puffing his chest out in her defense. "Torranze only built the rocket with your help."

"That's right," she replied, focusing all her thoughts on Zvin. "With my help, with your help, and with everyone else's help. He can't do it alone. We cannot stop now."

The two stood in a silence in which suddenly Edart could feel the presence of every quadar in the facility—all of them bent to some chore, all of them working now despite the fears that Zvin had voiced and that she knew to be true.

She felt the extra assignment that Torranze had given her as a presence in the room, too.

She wasn't an idiotic quadar.

She knew why Torranze and Crissandr were returning to Esgarat City. She knew what the smaller rocket and its launching tube were meant to do.

"It's going to mean a sacrifice, though," she finally said. "A greater sacrifice than Louratna envisioned."

Zvin gave a noncommittal chuff before the skin around his primaries softened. "All right," he said, raising one six-fingered hand. "I believe we can make it too. But not because of Torranze."

An almost painful amalgam of embarrassment and pleasure rose inside Edart as she understood what he was saying.

Zvin Tek put a hand to her shoulder.

Her hearts beat harder and her breath almost stopped.

"I believe in you, Edart Kel," he said. "If you say it can be done, I know it will be done."

"Thank you," she said.

He slid his hand down her arm to rest exquisitely above the elbow, his strong, curled fingers cupping the round of her arm. He paused then, as if gaining courage.

"I would like to spend time together if you would have me."

She felt him there beyond the pressure of his hand on her arm. Solid and unmoving. The heat was more than she could bear.

She felt hope then. Actual hope. The best kind of desperation, she thought. The sense that she had someone behind her.

"I would like that," she said.

His grip softened. Then he smiled.

"All right," he said with a bright voice. "But right now, I need to work on getting that extra support in place."

She smiled. "Dinnertime?"

He nodded. "That would be lovely."

He turned to his task.

Edart, too, moved to the next chore.

Now that the cleanup was progressing, she needed to get the smelting facility operational. She wanted to review a change to the assembly area that Torranze should have made even before the attack.

She wanted to talk to Janti, too, an older quadar she had worked with earlier to design the more intricate aspects of casting the body of the original rocket. Janti had come to the mountain from the

Festia Family—he was an expert in the trade. She didn't think the launch tube Torranze wanted would be a problem but, though intensely aware of her youth, she'd been designing equipment for long enough to know scaling down the rocket would be tricky.

Her head was spinning as she walked away.

And she was certain she could still feel warmth of Zvin's hand on her arm.

CHAPTER 16

Crissandr lay against the shade side of a *banka* tree, her back padded by the pack that was now half-empty, her worst leg propped on a rock. She held her arms out to capture the breeze and had her legs aligned to keep them in that same shade.

Eldoro had set a few minutes earlier, and Torrance could already feel the difference against his skin. Katon was still high enough in the sky that there would be light for about another hour.

It was their third break since going it on foot.

They had been moving only a short while since their last stop, and for several minutes Crissandr's chest heaved with a mix of exertion and pain.

"I've killed us," she said.

"You have done no such thing," Torrance replied once he understood her. "We are both struggling to maintain."

"I broke the cart," she replied.

Torrance wasn't going to let her dwell on the crash.

"Accident," he tried to say, though the only quadarti he knew for such a term translated as *mistake.* Though they were rapidly finding ways to share more bits of language, communications were still sometimes frustrating. "Could have been me," he added. "And I didn't say for you to stop."

Crissandr gave a spicy *piff* out of the side of her mouth. "I broke cart."

"No."

"I did."

They could go on like this for some time if he let it.

Fact was fact, though. He had to admit their trip—which was already going to have been a tough one—now carried more risk. Without the motor cart, and with Crissandr on a leg so gimpy she couldn't move without support, he felt out of sorts. They chose this path—down mountain, but high in the foothills—because it was comparatively comfortable and because enough vegetation still grew here that they could take cover as they rested. Their position now, sitting in the shade of the combination of a natural stone pillar and a gnarled *banka* tree, was a good example.

Its comfort was a double-sided favor, though.

The foliage and broken rock also provided ample cover for the wide mix of predators that roamed this high in the mountains.

Torrance had already chased away one such encounter, though that had been a half-hearted stalking by a smaller form of the feline *rela* beast. Torrance called it a mountain lion until Crissandr gave him the quadarti term *chikarel.*

Torrance eyed their remaining water skin.

It was barely half full now.

Crissandr pointed to the base of the *banka.* "There," she said.

Torrance groaned as he got to his feet.

His shoulder was stiffening, and his knee was tender where it had skimmed rock during their crash. He rotated his shoulder to loosen up. "Lucky I didn't break my collarbone," he said aloud.

"What?"

"Nothing," he said. "What did you want?"

She directed him to the tree's root system where, buried in dark cracks, he found a small patch of *kado.* His heart jumped.

"Oh, come here, you beautiful tuber you!"

He was worried about food. Last night he'd tried to trap a *piela* lizard, but had failed miserably. He knelt to clear loose dirt from the plant's base, then extracted it using a thick-bladed knife pulled from his boot. Digging through the dirt was easier up against the root system, but the *kado* had dug itself down deep and extracting it cost Torrance considerable effort. His fingers ached as he pressed them into the hole he created. Eventually he succeeded, though. The *kado* came out whole, including a network of tendrils that clung together to make it look like a mop head.

He cut it into parts and brought half to Crissandr.

The treat wasn't going to sustain them for long, but it was zesty and reinvigorating on Torrance's tongue.

"*Mata*," he said when he finished.

"*Mata,*" Crissandr replied.

"I thought *kado* only grew in rocky crevasses."

Crissandr smiled. "Little plants find their own shade."

Torrance nodded. "Survival of the fittest."

Crissandr's brow ridge wrinkled and central peeked open. "Survival of the persistent," she replied.

Torrance laughed.

"I suppose that's right, too."

"You need to go ahead," Crissandr said.

"Let's not do this again."

Crissandr raised the thick bramble stick she'd been using as a cane. "I cannot walk as we need to walk to arrive to Esgarat City. But you can. So, leave me. Go on forward."

"Seriously, let's not start that again," Torrance said.

"I will huddle here. You come back when you can."

"We both know you will die if you are alone out here." He paused, seeing her struggle with his words. "*Indati,*" he said, pointing to her. "Both know *indati.*"

"Both know you need to make it, also." She pointed a gnarled finger at his chest. "Need to find Baraq."

Torrance sighed.

"Neither of us are ready for this now," he said, telling the truth.

The tumble he'd taken had left him bruised and battered, too. If he hadn't needed to be strong for Crissandr, he wasn't sure he'd have made it this far, either.

"There's no reason to think I can make it there on my own right now either," he said. "We both need time to heal, so that's what we're going to do."

Her primaries tightened with an emotion Torrance read as something between anger and anxiety.

"How?"

"I don't know. We find a cave. Spend a few days. Maybe go in deep enough to condense water. Or just find roots."

"Wild caves are as dangerous as desert," Crissandr replied.

He smiled and raised his knife.

"I am dangerous, too."

She laughed, and Torrance felt better.

"Dangerous to roots, anyway," she finally said.

He laughed then.

"Yes," he said. "I am Torranze the Great, Maimer of all Tubers."

Her chest heaved with a half laugh of her own.

"What is *tuber*?"

"A root," he said. "But that doesn't matter. What matters is this: I've already lost Louratna. I'm not going to lose you. We'll make it work. That's all that matters. We'll make it together, or we won't make it at all."

He drew a sharp breath, hoping it was the former but worried that it might well be the last. When she gave her resigned capitulation, Torrance's gaze went up the mountain, searching for an opening that didn't exist there.

CHAPTER 17

This Eldoro down I will leave, Karshi Fael thought while sitting atop a flat disk of rock that jutted from a rugged cliff face. She peered up at the greater heat as Eldoro made his way to the top of his arc.

She had rested two heats now.

She was as ready as she would be.

The full weight of what this departure meant bore down on her. Was this the last time she would take in the high vista? The last time the mountain would be under her feet? The stone's warmth pressed against the thicker hide of her thighs. The winds were still sweet to her, despite the dust they carried.

She turned her gaze westward, toward Harshish Point.

Even if she discounted the intensity the greater heat had carried since the cloud cover had now all but burned away, she was getting too old to travel through the times of Eldoro peak.

Working the desert in full darktime had always been a danger of its own.

So Karshi decided she would begin each leg of her travels before Eldoro was setting, and then push hard while Katon was still casting her light. The challenge would be to find the proper spots to shelter—particularly in Eldoro highpoint—which it was now. The rising temperatures on the rock served as confirmation of her assessment. Her thin wrap was no defense against Eldoro's rays.

Karshi unstrapped a water skin, drank, then slid off the flat rock to find her way to take cover in the mountainside crevasse she'd been housing herself in.

She would sleep now and would leave when she woke.

CHAPTER 18

Survival of the fittest.

As he watched over Crissandr's sleep, Torrance remembered that line from their conversation earlier in the day.

He wondered about it.

Crissandr had replaced Darwin's findings with a different word, *persistence*, but, really, how much of a gap was there between the fittest and the most persistent?

He supposed he was splitting hairs.

Staring up at Katon—Alpha Centauri B to his human learning— as the lesser heat moved across the sky to chase Alpha Centauri A, he wondered how long anything living on this planet would last.

He imagined the star pattern above them.

Imagined a moving white gleam of a satellite's reflection. A starship's path.

The idea of spacecraft seemed so far away now.

That kind of technology felt like it had never been possible, like it had never existed. That it did, in fact, exist, pressed on him here in the silence of the small cavern he and Crissandr had found.

The rasp of her breathing, soft in the emptiness of the cave as she slept, felt intimate.

Assuming the wormhole gate was still feeding interstellar travel of his species back in the Solar System, how long would it be until A was so depleted of energy that it would kill off everything here?

Soon, he thought.

Sooner than he'd expected.

Eden was in the middle of the second stage of its death throes.

Heating up now, Eden's atmosphere was collecting all of Alpha Centauri A's heat as well as that of Alpha Centauri B. The star wouldn't keep up, though, and Katon's dim light—Alpha Cen B— would never be enough to sustain life alone.

No heat, no roots.

No roots, no food.

No food...

What would be left, then?

He'd long ago given up the idea of ever seeing the Solar System again himself, but he hadn't fully come to grips with what his people had done to the quadars on Eden. What plant or animal would be *persistent* enough to make it after the quadars were gone? Or would this second phase get so harsh that everything alive today would simply bake away before the ice age would come to claim them?

Torrance flexed his sore hands, feeling the presence of Louratna with him, imaging her stern expression of impatience.

He needed to succeed.

The original plan to seed the atmosphere with aerosols had been challenging enough, but he knew he needed to go farther now. Getting a rocket off the ground large enough that people in the Solar System would immediately recognize it carried a wide set of problems.

Logistics. Production. Navigation.

There would be more than technology to deal with, too.

The quadarti would need to work together—the entire community—to focus. Whatever skirmish Baraq was into, they would have to get through it soon.

He had to make it happen. He had to.

Time was short, though.

He needed to get a rocket off the ground soon.

A rocket with a message made clear.

At that thought, he gave a soft laugh that was more of an exhale. Talk about your kick in the pants. *I'd love to see the conference after they find it*, he thought.

CHAPTER 19

The first stage of Karshi Fael's expedition was uneventful. She picked her way carefully down the mountain and into the foothills where the vegetation grew sparse, and then—just prior to her darktime limit—into the desert fringe.

When Karshi found the *razo* carcass toward the end of her second stint—eaten through but still fresh enough that the kill had to have been recent—she decided to stop. *Neantha*, she thought, had been the culprits. The *razo* had been young enough to still be fleet of foot, which told her the beast had been hobbled in some fashion. Otherwise, the *neantha* pack that had taken it down had simply been lucky, or so desperate that they carried persistence onward beyond the norm.

Either was possible.

A healthy *razo* should be able to outdistance a pack here in the vast openness, though. And this animal was large enough that the pack which had taken her down had left chunks of meat clinging to its bones.

She knelt beside it, noting the trail of crawlers that ran to and from the carcass, then ran her finger along a still glistening rivulet of blood that clung to one of the *razo*'s exposed bones.

She lifted the liquid to her tongue. It tasted sharp, but robust.

She had already drunk more water than she'd planned on. The blood was good.

She would rest here, she thought.

She was tired.

The good tired, though.

Her mind had focused on the terrain for her long hike. Her senses had been on high alert the whole time, filled with sounds and scents that came of walking through brush grounds filled with scraggly foliage, and through ravines formed by the sudden rushes that came after rare rains. It was rugged ground, bone-dry and craggy. It would grow only more so as she made her way into the far desert.

Feeling Eldoro's intense heat, Karshi scanned the vast and cracked horizon to see if she could make out the pack. By the state of the carcass, they had left some time ago, but *neantha* were smart creatures—and not above hunting for sport as much as for feeding. She had seen packs double back before, returning to a carcass to see if they could grab another meal made of any scavenger attracted to their leavings.

Karshi saw only a small pack of *tal* beasts in the far distance, though, a cloud of dust following their slow movement toward the mountains.

She scanned again.

Nothing.

She knelt back to the carcass, knees up over her head as she considered her next steps.

To take the remains with her could be dangerous—*neantha* would follow a blood path if she left one behind. The meat would be sinewy. *Razo* was never to her taste, but only a foolish quadar left such a gift behind completely. She needed the sustenance as much as she needed to get out of the heat.

Karshi saw a broken crack a distance away.

Investigation proved it was deep enough to provide cooling shade and positioned such that she would be able to see danger approaching from a distance.

Fighting fatigue and the rising heat of Eldoro, she dragged the carcass to the crevasse's edge.

It was a short fall to the bottom.

Gauging the distance, she mumbled to herself. "Don't just drop it," she said. To simply toss the dead beast down the crevasse was disrespectful. Worse, it would threaten to damage what pelt remained. She planned to use the time before she slept to recover that skin—which she would employ to mend her worn *kami*, the leathered pants she had torn at both knees. If there was enough skin left, she could cure it to form into a new skin for water.

Deciding the safest route, she dragged the carcass further down the crevasse lip.

After resting a moment, she gave one huge push and slid the animal's remains over the edge.

It gave a slow half-tumble and half-slide down the slope.

Picking her way carefully, Karshi scaled the wall down, noting places that she could cup water out of the cooling air when that time came, and noting, too, a small patch of bramble growing near the bottom of the split. She would save her rations by eating that before sleeping.

Finally at the floor, she stretched herself in the cool shade.

The rock here still held the darktime chill.

She disrobed, and pressed herself against it—first the front, hugging the rock as if it were Karshi's long-lost sibling, which in a real sense she considered it to be.

"Thank you, stone," she said, feeling her skin open and the heat prickle away.

When she had cooled properly on that side, Karshi Fael turned to press her back to the rock, feeling the blood flow through her shoulder plates to trickle down into her chest.

As her body cooled, she felt her stomachs—which her body had shut down in the heats—returning to their functions.

She pulled a sharp knife from her belt and turned to the carcass.

CHAPTER 20

"This looks good," Edart Kel said, holding the hollow tube up to the ceiling like a telescope, then squinting into it. The device was deceptively weighty, but she was able to keep its momentum from making it fall from her hands. "Are you sure the new rocket will fit into it?"

"If the plans and sample you gave me are true," Janti replied.

"They are true."

"Then the casing will serve."

Edart put the hollow tube on the table and rolled it absently against her palm, sensing its perfect roundness.

"You do very good work, Janti."

"It makes me happy," the metalworker replied.

Edart watched as Janti returned the tube to its proper place. The quadar was as particular about his shop as he was precise in his work.

She was dead on her feet.

She couldn't remember if she'd eaten today.

No, that wasn't true. She was certain she'd had some dried *dashtar* and a cup of brewed *havra* root. Or was that last night? She couldn't remember.

It wasn't going to get any better anytime soon, either.

She had to go to the kitchen next to look at a newly fired oven that had cracked on first use. And the fueling station had been waiting on a repair too long, so she'd go there also, where, as

Torranze might have said, she might have to "kick some quadarti tail."

There was Zvin Tek, too.

She had promised to spend dinner times with him, but there was so little time that even when she could meet, she always left him feeling like she was running out on him. She had been unwise to begin such relations with Zvin, but he had made her feel things she had never felt before.

She let go a long breath, straightened, and took in the metalworker as he returned to her.

"I'm sorry to have interrupted your work, but this was the only period I could find to come down today."

"It is not a problem, Edart Kel," Janti replied. The older quadar was still in his metalwork togs, which were composed of a light tunic of rootcloth and a heavier protective upper made of *tal* leather. He still held the pair of thick gloves he wore while pouring the molten metals he used while casting. "I needed the break, and we all know the stresses you are putting onto yourself."

Edart didn't know what to say in response.

It was true.

She was pushing herself too hard.

"Thank you. I just want everything to be right when Torranze returns."

"At this rate you may get the rocket off the ground again by that time."

She laughed.

"Thank you again, Janti. Your spirit makes me happy."

"I'm not making fun. We all see it."

An awkwardness came over her, and Edart wasn't sure what to say. "Well," was all that came out of her mouth. Janti stood silently before her amid the steady rumbling of the smelting and casting operation.

Finally, after a more than awkward silence in which she knew he was staring at her, she met his gaze.

"Don't do that, Edart Kel," he said after their primaries locked.

"Do what?"

"Pretend that you don't know what you're doing."

"I'm—"

"I told you we all see it," Janti said in as stern of a voice as Edart could ever remember him using with her.

She stopped in her tracks.

"We know you are young. We do. I understand the sensations that must be going through you. You are not familiar with being responsible for other quadars, so you ignore it. But I'm not afflicted with your youthful oblivion. So, hear this now. Without what you are doing, it is likely the entire facility would be derelict now. But we see you. Look around. This whole place is running again, and without you … it wouldn't be. You can be humble without pretending this is not true."

Janti's praise fell over Edart like a cascade of clean rain.

Her skin tingled.

The moment stretched into an awkward silence again, but this time it felt different.

She had so much to do, but at the same time couldn't ignore that sense of pride that welled up inside.

"Thank you, Janti. I will try to do better."

"Try?" The elder laughed. "Everything is a task with you, eh, whelpling?"

"I guess."

She took a moment to look out over the operation.

Even with the ravages of the Family raid still in evidence, Janti's workplace was a thing of beauty. Precisely designed in its apparent randomness, from the mounds of presorted ores and metals on the intake side, to the slanted scoops that slid those ores into grinders, and the fire-heated trays where metal particles boiled into stream and slag—which were, in turn, separated into their own uses— everything had its place.

"You are an inspiration, too," she said. "No one else has completed their cleanup in such record time."

He waved his hand to shrug off the comment. "I was lucky."

There was a small amount of truth in that. Janti *had* been lucky that his initial staging consisted of mineral-laced ore. At the time the Families had attacked, the operation had just received another load from miners deeper in the complex, and three mounds of that rubble helped shield the most important of the machined smelting trays.

Still, the layout had been perfect.

"Luck has nothing to do with your design," she said.

He shrugged again.

"All right," she said, motioning the tube. "That's enough of our mutual admiration society. Can we test it tomorrow?"

"I don't see why not. Assuming the rocket is ready, anyway."

Edart gave a twitch of her left primary. She was having issues scaling the technology down, but what they had was good enough for a simple integration trial.

"It will be ready enough."

"Then we should be able to give it a run."

"Excellent."

Edart left the chamber then, feeling glances from the workers around her, walking with a renewed energy and a greater sense of purpose than she'd felt in the heats since Torranze had left.

Perhaps, she thought, she *could* get that rocket off the ground before he returned.

CHAPTER 21

A guttural grunt startled Karshi Fael from her sleep.

She gasped and gripped the knife she'd been holding, seeing a dark form bent down over the carcass.

Neantha.

It was a *neantha*, large and muscular, maw buried into the carcass, ears peeled backwards to sense danger. Everything snapped into place then. The dusty smell of the animal. The dark, mottled fur that stuck out from its hunched shoulders and angled back. The vivid sheen of rock that faded away behind the beast. Wind whistled over the chasm's mouth above her. The tearing sound of the beast's strong jaws ripping meat preceded it raising its head to swallow its dinner down its gullet, dark grime coating its teeth and tongue.

The *neantha*'s gaze centered on Karshi, then.

For a moment she worried the knife would be both necessary and inadequate. Instead, the beast returned to the flesh, leaning back against the remains of a leg until that leg cracked away from the main mass.

The *neantha* dragged the trophy a short distance away, then used its forelegs to brace the bone and rip even more shreds.

The animal was large, Karshi confirmed as her senses settled.

It smelled of danger.

It was alone, too, Karshi decided after a quick glance around, old, or injured so badly that the pack had abandoned it. She'd seen it before—a lone animal, left alone. The hunch of the *neantha's* body and the matted nature of its pelt made her fall on *old*, though.

The carcass had drawn it, but the idea that the beast might have come across her anyway left Karshi to imagine what would have happened if the easier meal wasn't available.

She shouldn't have fallen asleep.

Not here, anyway.

Not now.

Light slanted across the crevasse at a sharp enough angle that the *neantha* cast a hard-edged shadow against the floor and far wall of the shaft. It said Eldoro was falling but was still high in the sky.

Not wanting to startle the animal, she pulled her legs slowly toward herself, then sat up so she would have leverage if the beast attacked. She felt hard rock against her back and against the hand she used to balance the movement.

Her stomachs churned as she watched the animal, but Karshi felt stronger as each moment settled.

She didn't want to lose the carcass, but the desert takes as well as it gives. She'd been lucky enough to find the carcass before the blood turned muddy, and at least she had the skins that, once properly prepared, would make a good water vessel.

She watched the animal eat.

If the *neantha* ate its fill, it might leave her be.

As she waited she thought about the desert itself, for the first time truly contemplating what it might mean to die out here in the nowhere of its harsh sands—to become foodstuff for the *neantha*, or the *rela*, or to simply be buried under the sands perhaps to sometime become the pickings for the soaring *jah* that she now saw circling in the open dome above them or the crawlers that still made their way in lines to the dead *razo*.

It would be a good death. That was her first thought.

She'd been whelped in the outer regions of these savage plains. As she watched the *neantha* devour its meal, Karshi realized for the first time that it only made sense that she would return to them.

Just not now, though.

Truth was she'd been dreading this trip for several cycles. It would be a long trip, and a hard one. Her body was older now. Stiffer and less reliable. She hadn't ventured out this far in some time, but she was certain enough of her need to avoid lying to herself. Her body needed more rest than it once did. She had planned a laggardly pace that wouldn't tax her so much, but that meant she wouldn't arrive at Harshish Point for several more heats.

Watching the *neantha* gnaw on the leg, listening to the bone-sharp crack of the *razo*'s remains falling to the strength of the *neantha*'s jaws, Karshi Fael sat and waited, gripping her knife tightly and deciding most certainly that she did not want to die today.

CHAPTER 22

"It has been five heats, Torranze. I am as ready as I have to be,"
Crissandr said. "We go again when Eldoro fades."

"I don't think so," Torrance said as she teetered on her best leg.
"You could use another heat to rest."

"No choice. We are out of water. I can walk."

Torrance couldn't pretend it wasn't true.

Crissandr was as obstinate as Louratna had been about certain
things, too. He'd been lucky enough to get her to rest and recover
for this long only because the extent of her injuries was so obvious
that she couldn't ignore them.

She lowered herself back to sit against the far wall of the
crevasse they'd found, five meters deep into the mouth. She still
used their empty pack as padding against the rugged surface. He
glared at her and she propped her foot up on a rock.

Torrance, legs crossed, sat across from her, bent forward to
focus on his task—which was using a carved needle and a length of
twined skin of the *piela* lizard they'd eaten earlier to mend a hole
in his trousers. If there was a positive to this stoppage, it was that
Crissandr had spent her past five heats schooling him on certain
facts of living in the wild on Eden, not the least had been how to
make the thread he was using now.

Crissandr was pragmatic to a fault.

She'd used her down time to teach him how to trap more
effectively, and how to find hard roots in places he'd have never

expected to find them in. And he'd done these with expertise enough that at least they'd eaten without digging into their stores.

Water was a different situation altogether.

Crissandr taught him how to capture lifegiving blood from the creatures they trapped. She'd helped him dress their catch and taught him how to cook it in ways better than simply searing the hell out of it—to wrap it in the thicker leaves of the hearty foliage that grew outside the mouth of the cave, and thereby hold onto the meat's natural juices. She'd shown him how to find plants that stored liquid—and others that leached water from what little cooling humidity there was here.

It was never going to be enough, though.

"We need to find another cave," he finally said. "One that runs to water."

He stared out the cave mouth, seeing harsh orange and brown lands splayed in the distance below. The greater heat was nearing its peak, bringing waves to the air that warped the horizon in blankets oppressive enough to feel even from this far into the cave. A billowing ball of haze rose from a spot far on the horizon—a dust storm, he thought. A burning wind, as the quadarti called it.

It was oddly beautiful, swirling in the distance, but it also raised fear he felt in the hair along his arms.

A full-forced wind here was powerful enough it could scour a quadar to the bone if that quadar was foolish enough to face it head-on.

The terrain outside the cave wasn't without its peril.

He worried Crissandr wasn't ready. Even staying on the natural trail, it would be a harsh trip. But they needed water.

The decision wasn't good either way.

"Perhaps we travel a day then rest a day?" Torrance offered.

Crissandr twisted a corner of one lip up in that particularly quadarti expression that told him she was deflecting.

"Perhaps not."

He laughed.

She *humpfhed* from the back of her throat and raised two fingers.

"Will be better to two-go."

"Two-go?"

"Walk from Eldoro fade to Katon set, then rest in the darktime, and walk again from Eldoro rise to Katon rise."

"Then rest through Eldoro high?"

"Yes," she said. "*Mata*. This time of cycle two-go."

He pressed his lips together, realizing how much time there was between Eldoro high to the moment the quadars called Eldoro fade—when the greater heat was four hands from setting. He hadn't been ready to leave so quickly, better yet as often as she was presenting.

"Will your ankle bear that kind of effort?"

"We go," she said firmly as if to say his concerns no longer mattered. "This heat. Go as Eldoro fades."

"All right," Torrance said, raising his hands to show his full capitulation. He'd truly had been lucky to convince her to stay put these five heats.

There would be no going back now.

Outside the cave, heat rolled in from the baked ground to warm his face and arms. The sensation recalled a time when he was with Marisa and leaning over an open oven—a snippet of a time so far in the past now—when they'd worked together to make a birthday cake.

He glanced back at Crissandr, then back to the open desert.

Crissandr was right.

It was time to go.

But this was not going to be a cakewalk.

And Torrance worried.

CHAPTER 23

The shadows had crawled a full hand up the crevasse wall when it became obvious the *neantha* had eaten its fill. It gave a whine of satisfaction, then padded carefully to a shaded nook across from Karshi, where it gave a cautious turn and, with golden-orange eyes focused on Karshi, dropped itself to the ground with a sudden thud.

It lay there, panting for several beats.

Wind played its music above her.

The animal's smell came to Karshi, dusky and covered in the metallic tones of clotting blood.

Another hand later, she began to get nervous.

Karshi had expected the beast to move on once it had finished its meal, but instead it lowered its head to its front legs and began to doze.

She wanted to be on the move again but didn't want to startle the beast into an attack.

Eventually, the *neantha* seemed to enter a full sleep.

Karshi's first instinct had been right.

The beast was older. A female. Its pelt, mottled with clumps of fur balled into knots, told Karshi that the herd had not groomed this animal in some time. She was right then, to peg the *neantha* as an outcast. The tips of its fangs, one chipped, were yellow-brown pikes that grew from her upper lip.

When the shadows grew another hand's distance over the rocky wall, Karshi began to think she might be able to slip away.

Slowly she stood.

The *neantha* stirred, opening one orange-gold eye to take her in.

The animal's eyes closed again.

Even more slowly, Karshi reached her pack and her stick, then slid the knife back into her belt. The beast raised its head to watch her movements with as much intensity as Karshi had watched its dinner.

When she had gathered herself, Karshi gave the beast a gentle nod. "Be well," she said to it softly. Then she climbed up the rock face, slowly, watching for movement, until she could slide a leg over the edge and raise herself up.

She glanced down one more time, then walked away, softly still, always watching the cliff's edge and pulling the knife closer again in case it was necessary.

A moment later, with a grunt and the heavy sound of deep breathing, the *neantha* made a leap from farther down the crevasse where the climbing had been easier. When it noticed Karshi's attention—saw her standing poised with the stick and the knife both at hand, the beast held its position, staring at her. Its eyes glowed golden in the last of Eldoro's light. They went wide, then narrowed and then widened again.

Still facing the beast, Karshi took another step backward, then another and another.

The *neantha*, too, edged along, following Karshi's path, stopping when Karshi stopped, and following again when Karshi moved.

"Are you joining me?" she said aloud.

The *neantha* whined and dropped its head.

"I don't have another *razo*."

The *neantha* was silent, but again followed Karshi when she moved on.

VIGILANTE

CHAPTER 24

The following darktime, Baraq Waganat left an Elganjo Family store in pieces. It had been an operation of chance rather than anything he had planned, but it fed into his sense of vengeance.

He felt good leaving it in shambles.

The Family owned the rights to ceramics and pottery that, in normal times, the community used for cookware and other such equipment. Breaking it all gave him release. Crashing bowls to the floor made his hearts pump. Breaking vases and utensils gave him shivers. At one point he felt Brada beside him, recalled eating Crissandr's *havra* together on a piece of pottery that resembled the plates he was smashing.

The cracking of ornately fired decanters crumbling filled his hearts. The sensation of grinding dusty rubble under his feet as he left the shop was a physical thing that vibrated down deep into his bones. The sense of release he had while stepping into the darkness nearly made him scream with joy.

The next darktime Festia equipment burned again.

Then Pew'tal the next.

It was, he thought as time passed, not much.

The Elganjo Family were wealthy enough but, as most of the Kandar clan, were not one of the major brokers on the Council. They had five other outlets, too, so to take them down completely would have required five of him and a good deal of coordination—and if he knew anything beyond all other things it was that there was only one of him.

The loss of the Festia grinder didn't set them back at all. And the Pew'tal would restock quickly.

Nothing he was doing seemed to matter, the damage nothing worse than simple *piela* bites that healed over with a few heats' diligence. Yet, with each action he remembered Brada's body, lying in its bloody pool on its rocky dais. The image burned inside, his grief wrapped in a cloak of despair that came because he knew he wasn't helping anything. The Families were drawing harder lines. *Hedgie* families were no better off.

He would have to do more.

The events of those evenings cemented his path, though.

There was, he found, a magnificent sense of freedom that came from giving himself completely to something bigger than his own existence.

He was alone now.

He had nothing but his body and his sense of justice.

The Families had taken everything from him.

It would take time, but he would take as much from them.

CHAPTER 25

After another session of the Orange Ring, Ezi found little Pella exactly where she always did: Sitting at the edge of a cliff face and chattering to herself.

She had come to tell Pella she was going to travel back to the city tomorrow, that she was going to carry the Ring's decision to parlay with the Banit Family with her. Pella would take the news poorly, she knew. The whelp was feeling alone now. Isolated after all her losses and discarded now that Ezi was spending so much time with Orange Ring business.

Ezi was not an elder quadar, but the sight of Pella's thin contours against the open sky made the weight she felt even heavier.

The whelp's bony elbows jutted from the thin overwrap she wore to protect herself from Eldoro's heat, resting on knees she had levered up to her chest, feet and toes hugging the cliff edge. The garment was of a soft, dusky hue, open to expose her small central backplate, its skin recently cracked and peeled with growth to leave it smooth and gray in the way of youth. Her face had become more angular over the passing heats. Her lips were fleshing out.

Ezi peered through the dimmer light of evening down at the city of Esgarat, so far away that she could not discern movement of any type.

Pella's rambling chatter felt like a song to Ezi.

It was one, she supposed. A rhythm that played in the currents of air that rose from below.

It felt happy, in a way. Hopeful despite the direness of the moment.

The whelpling's expression was hard to decipher, though.

Her central was opened wide as if to sense heat contours from the desert out beyond the city, and her primaries were not quite closed. It was growing late down in the city, and the air in the mountains was growing cooler. The greater heat of Eldoro had just fallen below the horizon and was still casting a crimson flare across the domed sky. Lesser Katon, trailing, added in oranges and yellows from her higher perch. The combination painted pink crescents over the curves of Pella's smooth face.

It made Ezi wish she could sit down, stroke Pella's head, and let her rest on Ezi's shoulder while Ezi whispered to her: *Slow down, child,* she would say. *Take your time. Use your moments as they come.*

That would be wrong, though.

The world would not give this generation time to be playful, and Pella had already seen the Families' brutality up close.

Ignoring the desire to comfort Pella, Ezi came forward and took a place beside her, pulling at her shift to give her legs room, and wrapping her arms around her knees as she brought them upward to match Pella's pose.

"What will happen to my Baraq?" little Pella said.

Ezi chuffed, uncertain what to say about her thoughts on Baraq. She hadn't been prepared for the question, though she should have been. Pella had fed Baraq for many heats, bringing him food when he was Tierra's captive. She and Baraq had a closer relationship than Ezi usually considered. It was only natural Pella would think of him. Still, Ezi didn't want to jump to conclusions. Sister Vareta had not been wrong to point out her age. Ezi worried about Pella's ability to cope.

She took a deep breath of mountain air to help stifle the uncertainty she felt. "What do you mean?"

"He is late returning from his trip to the mountains."

"Yes, he is."

Ezi hadn't wanted Baraq to go to Louratna's. She had argued against it. The risk was too high, she'd said. They needed him here to continue Brada's work. Needed him to carry on Lelo's legacy—

the legacy of Baraq's own son.

That had been her argument.

The truth was deeper, though. She needed Baraq here to lean on after losing Brada. The pain she felt was like a hole burned so deeply into her chest that she didn't know if she could go on. Brada had been her pair-mate in every sense. She knew in her heart there would never be another.

He had been firm, though. *Louratna can help us*, Baraq had said. *I have to try.*

So, he had gone to the mountains to convene with Louratna, and now he was late returning, which could mean many dreadful things and no good ones. Ezi didn't know how to handle everything she was feeling about him, better yet how to convey it to this young whelpling who had also already lost so much and yet was still so full of questions.

The young quadar simply sat, though, uncrossing her legs to dangle them over the ledge of the steep cliff face below as she waited for answers.

"The way ahead is hard to see," Ezi said. "The Families will not treat him well if they manage to capture him. You've seen that as closely as any of us."

"I hope he is alive."

Ezi felt Pella's body heat as the young quadar leaned against her. For a moment, she wanted to tell Pella of her expectation: that Baraq was dead in the mountain raid, and that there was a reason to hope that this was true. Better dead than suffer what the Waganats could do when properly motivated. She held her tongue, though, finding nothing to gain from drawing such a line. The fact that Pella held such hope brought a ball of pain to Ezi's throat.

What if Baraq was not dead?

What if he was in the mountains, working to return?

"I miss his stories," Pella added. Baraq had told her stories during that captivity—the first being one about Lelo.

"I miss them, too," Ezi said, feeling intimacy in the response.

"When he returns will there be a fight?"

"You mean a war?"

"Yes," Pella said. "That's what I mean."

Her tone said she was overwriting language inside her mind, differentiating the term *fight* from the term *war*, and understanding the magnitude of their differences.

"I think it depends."

"On what?"

"On what he finds, and what he brings back."

Pella raised her hand so that her thin fingers cupped her skull. Her dangling feet pounded against the rocky face below.

Ezi gazed downward, calculating the drop to the jagged rock below as painful, knowing Pella deserved a better answer.

She pressed her eyes closed. Everything was so hard now. "I wish Brada were still here," she said. The words left her mouth as if they were weights. It was the first time she'd voiced that specific feeling to another quadar.

"I wish he were here, too," Pella said.

Pella put her little hand on Ezi's knee.

The mountain seemed to breathe with them for a few beats, and Ezi felt close to Brada again. For a moment, anyway. Sitting in the quiet, she could almost feel the touch of his hand and remember the gentle way his gaze caressed her when their eyes locked.

Crissandr was there in the mountains, too—living under Louratna's protection.

She would have gone too if she were Baraq. Nothing would have kept her away from her pair-mate.

She let her primaries take in young Pella.

Saw the curves of her face and the strength of her expression. The moment took her breath. What might their whelplings have been like? What would their lives together have yielded?

"You are going to be a strong quadar," she finally said.

Pella raised both ridges and pressed her lips together. "I want to be a strong quadar now."

Ezi saw it then. Pella was still unhappy with the Ring.

"I do not want to ever lie to you, Pella. So, I need to do a better job answering your question earlier."

Pella sat back. "Which question?"

Ezi chuffed.

"I don't know. All of them."

Pella craned her head to give full attention.

Ezi steeled herself. "No matter how Baraq returns, and even if he does not return, there will almost certainly be some kind of fighting," she said. "That is what our Orange Ring is discussing now. How to react. Who we need to connect with to help All of Esgarat. The Families will carve up the remains of the council, and then we'll see what happens. But if Baraq—or anyone else, for that matter—can bring hope from the mountains, the worst might be avoided."

"That would be good."

Ezi clicked to say she agreed. "That may not be the way things happen, though. It could get bad."

"How bad?"

Ezi put her hands palm up.

The cooler air was starting to feel sharp.

In the distance a pair of *jah* began their hunt.

"Fear motivates the Families now, Pella. They worry they are losing power, and you've seen how brutal they can be when faced with losing their power."

"If Baraq does not return, will you take Brada's place as Lelo?"

That Pella had asked the question meant she understood both the separation of Brada and Lelo, as well as how the loss of Lelo could foretell the death of something important. Ezi considered her response.

"I don't know if anyone can take Lelo's place."

"But you will lead them, like you've led the gathering."

"I will do my best to help any quadar who needs help."

Pella gave an absent click. Her gaze followed the two *jah* as they rode a high current.

"I will do my best too," Pella replied with an earnest intensity.

"I know you will."

Ezi put her arm around Pella's shoulder and drew her tight. She knew then what she had to do.

"That's why I need to ask you a favor."

"What is it?"

"At Eldoro rising, I am going to take a trip. I would like you to come with me."

"A trip?"

"The Ring has decided we are going to speak with the Banit Family. I would like you to be there when we go. I think you can help."

"Then I'll go."

Ezi smiled, hoping she'd done something good. A few moments

later Ezi stood and brushed down her shift as it settled.

"Come," she said to Pella. "It is time for supper."

"I'm not hungry."

"You are a growing quadar," Ezi said, trying to get her tone of admonishment right. "Besides, the Ring will likely still be discussing plans."

A tinge of anticipation came to Pella's expression then.

Her primaries expanded, and both ear flaps turned upward so imperceptibly that Ezi might have missed it if she weren't concentrating on the whelpling.

"All right," Pella said, lifting a hand so Ezi could help her to her feet. "Do we have any *dashtar* fruits?"

"We will have to see," Ezi said. "I don't want to promise something I can't make happen."

She took Pella's hand and raised her up.

"I hope we do," she said.

"Me, too," Ezi said.

The two strode back into the network of caves.

There was work to do. Preparations to be made.

CHAPTER 26

Early darktime, Baraq came across an alleyway and a gang of Tegra enforcers beating a lesser quadar.

"I did it! I did it! I cleaned the floor! I did it!" the quadar called out as blows fell in thick *whumpfs*.

"Give it back," one of the three Tegras said, breath raw and ragged under the effort of the beating.

Baraq understood, then.

This was a shakedown. The Tegras had paid this *hedgie* for his work, and now the guards wanted that pay back.

With the gang fully engaged in their fun, Baraq was able to approach closely.

"I think you've got the wrong idea," he said in a firm voice.

The three Tegras whirled to find him standing a close distance away, gun trained on them.

"I would hate to use your own Family's weapon against you," he said. "But don't think I won't."

The fight was quick.

Baraq ducked one blow, then shot.

A Tegra thug went down, and the other two ran.

It was only in that moment of still aftermath when the entire world went quiet that Baraq saw the whelpling who was cowering in an alcove.

"Lelo," the youth said.

The world around them came back to life, sounds of the city responding to the retort of the shot. Baraq felt the weight of the gun and smelled the aroma of fresh blood in the alley. The Tegra lay still, cooling in the darkness.

The battered quadar got to his feet, wheezing with the effort.

"Lelo," the youth said again.

"No," Baraq said, backing away, his hearts pounding with his son's name. "I'm not Lelo."

"Lelo!" the elder quadar said, grasping at Baraq's arm as he tried to stand. "You've come back!"

"Lelo!" the boy called again, this time louder and more forceful.

Baraq yanked his arm from the grasp.

"No," he spat, then he turned to the whelp. "Get your father back home," Baraq said. "You should not be out this late."

Then he turned and ran into the darkness.

CHAPTER 27

The heat was growing short, and Ezi was tired. The travels down the mountain and into the outskirts of Esgarat City had already been both long and frustrating, but time was as short as the heat. She wanted to get this over with now.

What she didn't want, as they made their way across the rich Banit land to consult with their Family's elder patriarch, was to add "deal with whelplings" into the mix of things that were drawing her attention. Alas, that did not seem possible.

"Pella," she said sharply before they were within earshot.

"I'm tired," the young quadar said.

"Behave or I'll not bring you with me again."

That quieted her for the moment.

She realized now that she should have left Pella with the rest of their traveling party, but her pride had gotten the best of her. The rest of the leadership ring had argued against Pella's participation, but Ezi wasn't taking no for an answer this time. To get this far and then leave Pella behind would have felt like losing. Too much was at stake though, and as the two of them approached the Banit leader, she hoped her argument—that having a whelpling with her would make for a better conversation with a Family that was certainly known for their love of younger quadars—turned out to be true.

Ezi took Pella's hand and held it tightly as she came across the fields to stand before Usatalto Banit, the Banit elder, who was standing knee-deep in freshly tilled and wetted sand.

"Welcome to this property," said the Banit.

Everything about him, from the hand rakes and scoopers that dangled from the toolbelt he wore looped around his waist to the heat-scarred shoulders of his muscular upper body, spoke of manual labor. Yellow mud caked his forearms and hands. His face crinkled with a combination of age and exposure that suggested he'd been in this field for ages. "I beg your forgiveness for my state," he added. "But one must work while the timing provides."

"Greetings to you, Master Banit," Ezi said. "I am honored to gain your time."

"Usatalto," he called. "We are not in the council chambers, so I prefer a simple name."

Ezi took a moment to gaze over the open horizon.

One advantage of seeing the Banit Family rather than any other was that, by necessity, the Family lived away from the towers and bustle of the city. Those buildings loomed in the distance, though, clouded by an orange haze of dust. The sight of the buildings so close made her feel an edge of danger, but for as far as she could see in all other directions there was nothing but open land and bowled sky.

Several other quadars were working the same pit as Usatalto, and more were in adjacent such plots.

An aroma thick with organics covered the area.

She breathed a tired, but good breath.

"Perhaps things would be better if you offered to hold all the council chamber's sessions out here."

The Banit patriarch gave a loud, clicky laugh.

"If nothing else maybe we'd actually get something done."

He made his way to the edge of the pit.

"*Pella, stop that,*" Ezi said as she noted the whelp bending at the edge of the pit and pulling a clod of wet mud up.

Pella craned her gaze upward.

"I brought you here because I thought you were ready. Please don't infringe on our host's property."

Usatalto clicked again.

"It is good to get to know your home," he said. "Let her play in the Esgarat."

Ezi felt at once chastened by the elder Banit's lesson and

encouraged by his obvious love for the whelplings.

"Come," Usatalto said to Pella. He twisted his frame and called out across the fields. "Anko! Come!"

She had seen the Banits on several occasions before, but not enough to have picked out one of their youngest. Still, a youth came forward, covered in so much mire that Ezi wouldn't have recognized him as a Banit if it weren't for Usatalto's call.

"Take young Pella to the first pit," he said. "Give her a treat and then show her how to seed."

"Yes, *Apa*."

Pella gazed at the elder Banit with wide eyes.

"You don't mind getting a little dirty, do you, young quadar?"

"No," she said with a tone of excitement that made Ezi feel suddenly sad.

"Thank you," she said to Usatalto after the two had left. "The little one so much wants to be useful."

The elder Banit extricated himself from the pit, then stood tall, not taking time to dispossess himself of the clots of wetted soil that slowly streamed down his torso and legs.

"The young can always be helpful."

Ezi nodded, feeling vindicated she had won her case to bring Pella along.

"What can the Banit Family do for you, Ezi of the Orange Ring, once pair-mate of Brada?"

The comment was more assessment than formality, though she wasn't sure whether it was her continued association with the Orange Ring or her past with Brada that was of concern. Or both.

"I am not ashamed of who I am."

"I do not ask you to be. Still the question stands. What can we do for you?"

"Since you know who I am, you must know why I am here."

Usatalto gave a weary exhale.

"Your Orange Ring is failing and you wish me to join you."

"No," she said. "Though that would be welcome if you had such inclination. What I would like is for you to allow us to contribute to your workforce."

Usatalto waited, knowing there was more.

"I want to work with you so that we could set aside enough root stock and fruit yield to ensure the *hedgie* population are able to survive."

This time his click was softer and less specific.

"I am serious," Ezi said.

"As has been every Family who has been here before you. I may be a simple quadar of the Esgarat myself, but I'm not blind to the moment."

"I see. You'll give the Families aid though they have no workers but leave us to fend for ourselves."

"I did not say that."

"Then what are you saying?"

When Usatalto did not reply, she saw something deeper in his gaze. A sadness. A regret. She saw the depths there, too. She saw that Usatalto Banit understood the politics of the moment as well as anyone else. The Banit Family was a loyal and close Family. If needed, they would fight together, and they could cause pain. But they were not a war-faring Family.

In a real fight, they would lose.

Ezi looked to where Anko and Pella were working a pit together.

"We will work with you," Ezi said. "We will fight with you, too."

He laughed.

"I don't think you can win against the Families, Ezi of the Orange Ring, but I trust you. You care in the right places. I would not be afraid to throw my lot together with yours if I thought it would matter. What I am saying, though, is that I cannot give you what you want—even as you offer to pay in bloodwork."

"Because?" Ezi clicked in the inquisitive.

"The land is changed."

"Changed?"

"Look around you, Ezi of the Orange Ring." The elder Banit opened his mud-caked arms to gesture across the fields. They were not empty, but also not fertile—not filled with thick root as they would normally be. "The burning rains coiled every root it touched. Now the heats wither the rest. We will be fortunate if we have enough to give the Families this season. Next season will be worse."

Usatalto described how the Banits had ensured each pit was of a specific size and had laid each in precise geometric patterns, with rows seeded in a variety of compounds. This configuration allowed them to determine the results of several pairings against each other.

Ezi took him in, noting that the muds were already solidifying to a shell over his shoulders.

"These pits are your laboratories," she said, suddenly understanding what she had been watching.

"Yes," he replied.

"Where you learn how to best feed that land."

"Yes."

"Teach us, then," she said, suddenly desperate in ways she was only beginning to grasp. "The Banit Family has tuned itself to the land. Teach us so we can make our own."

"That is not how this works. The Banit Family has spent many generations honing this skill. If we give it away, we have nothing."

Ezi began to argue, but Usatalto held up two hands to stop her.

"But even then, even if we discounted all of that, I've told you it would not matter. Despite all our work in the pits, the land loses its ability to provide."

"You believe the land loss is permanent?"

"Nothing we do is helping."

Then she did see. Truly.

The quadarti had long ago "solved" the water problem. Well enough, anyway. At least the series of pumps and manually staffed stations worked to bring water from the depths into the city itself. And the use of a shared water source had helped draw All of Esgarat together—or at least made for the one situation wherein the average quadar understood the idea of community property well enough not to commit suicide by destroying everyone else's opportunity to survive.

Death for one was death for all.

But if the land was dying, all the rest was a farce.

Even supplying the Families was a short game.

"So you see why I cannot help you, Ezi of the Orange Ring, though to the depths of three hearts I wish that I could."

"Yes," she said. "I see."

A short while later she had gathered Pella up again, and the two made their way off the Banit lands.

Their resting place for the evening was a rounded rock that Ezi had noticed on their way here, a slab that jutted at an angle to give shelter from the earliest of Eldoro's rays.

They ate root, then settled.

Pella, still coated in the mire of a Banit pit, told Ezi about how Anko had showed her how to ensure a seed was both deep enough and shallow enough in the ground, and had explained to her how proper pruning of a *dashtar* made for the sweetness to change in the fruit.

Ezi, steeped in the knowledge that nothing she did would ever matter, nodded as she listened.

Tomorrow, she thought as she dozed fitfully after Pella had finally tired, they would go back to the gap the Orange Ring called home.

After that, she had no predictions.

CHAPTER 28

Baraq Waganat—sitting in a row with *hedgies* who were mostly looking for work—pried his central gently open. The wall he leaned against was rough, unpainted mudbrick. He sat draped in a ratty robe with his back against that wall, arms crossed along his belly and knees pulled up toward his chin.

It was midheat.

There was no work here, but Baraq didn't care about that. His purpose was to hide in plain sight and plan his next exercise—which he hoped would happen later this darktime.

The open plain of a "factory" lay before him.

It was a wide area, open to the sky, mostly flat, and defined by a tangled fence of sharp wire that surrounded it. The back side of the grounds opened to the wildlands that lay between the city and the lowest foothills of the mountains.

Just inside that far opening, workers had piled mounds of various root harvests that smelled of fresh soil and various vivid flavors.

Several other stations were scattered over the area, too—places where those mounds of hard root and gnarled wood were treated, cleaned, stripped of irregularities, and eventually packed up to be transported to other Family factories that would then convert the material into even more viable products.

The Jaw'l Family had controlled these works for the past five cycles, having wrested the license from the council through both hard negotiation and outright coercion.

Baraq's lips pursed at memories of that takeover.

It had happened just before his time on the council, but he heard rumors and recalled stories. Rumors said knifepoint had something to do with it, and the one time he'd opened his mouth to ask about the Jaw'l acquisition his father had stared him down hard enough he had understood not to go further. Having seen the council work since then, it didn't take him any real effort to imagine the process.

That was yesterday's wind, though.

All that mattered now was that by owning the processing of roots and shrubbery, and by the decisions the Jaw'l Family had made to then form their product into a wide range of the materials that other Families used to create products *they* owned, the Jaw'l Family had put themselves into the position of being a nexus. To disrupt Jaw'l production was to disrupt Ombat textiles and Denari construction, as well as the work of Kat'all, M'ktal, and Otara Families.

The idea made Baraq happy.

Break one link, break them all.

The barrel of the small gun pressed hard against his hip, raising the sense of purpose he felt as he searched the operation for weaknesses. In retrospect, he wished he'd grabbed a second smaller weapon rather than just the four-shooter. Smaller was better in his way of working. The four-shooter was more problem than it was worth.

Through the robe, he let his fingers touch the weapon.

He focused on that intake zone—that plot of land closest to the wild lands.

Noted another area down by a plot where workers soaked longer, more sinewy root stock in an acid bath to break down certain fibers and leave the ropy stock pliable.

Those vats were important. He knew that much from a tour Kadan Jaw'l had given him several cycles ago. *"Take the stock out too early and the root is hard to work, leave it in too long and the acid eats it to nothing,"* Kadan had said as he marched Baraq past the area.

Cycles on the council had given Baraq ample time to understand the Jaw'ls, but it had taken only a few moments to realize he didn't like them. They had always been hard to work with, and too firm with their workers. It was a combination that made Baraq uncomfortable.

By his count, there were four acid vats.

If he could get in early enough, he would have time to fill all four. Alternatively, he thought, his four-shooter could damage the vats enough to drain them all—thereby putting the facility out of operation for considerably longer than the single day that destroying one lot might accomplish. Maybe that weapon would have value after all.

He wished he'd retrieved bombs from the Tegras.

Explosives would make that work even easier.

He shifted his robe in the heat.

Next time.

Across the open grounds, a boss monitor cracked a whip to drive workers harder to the task of sorting the root stacks.

Baraq gave an involuntary grunt at the ferocity of the action.

The smell of blood came.

The work was hard and the compensation minimal, but still these *hedgies* lined up to do it.

Baraq grimaced from under his hood as his grumble drew attention from the quadar beside him.

The quadar froze as he gazed at Baraq.

"Lelo?" the voice came, bending lower.

"No," he said, motioning dismissal with one hand.

"Lelo!" the quadar called. "Lelo!"

The call seemed to flow over the rows of *hedgies*. "Lelo?" he heard over and over.

Gazes came from nearby.

A heat of fear rose in him. Recognition was death, he thought. Recognition brought attention, and attention ruined everything.

"No," he said. "Not Lelo."

But the gathering was already growing agitated, and among the gazes the activity had drawn were those of the Jaw'l guards—a group Baraq most definitely did not want to draw attention from.

His chest froze with fear.

He did not want to find out what Family guards would do to a frenzied mass of *hedgies* who were chanting for Lelo.

In a single motion, he stood and pushed his way down past the job line to the street, finally emerging into the open only to have a few of the quadar pack follow him.

"Stop," they said. "Lelo! Stop!"

But Baraq kept moving, knowing that this job—no matter how attractive—was now blown.

CHAPTER 29

Jee El swallowed the last of the watered down *aska* he'd bought from a vendor up-street. In normal times he'd have beaten the vendor for the inferior quality of his product, but everything about him now, from his ragged clothing to his meek demeanor, had to be about blending in—something that was hard enough for him due to his size alone. Breaking the vendor's skull would serve no good purpose.

Instead, he worked on maintaining things he'd learned how to do—keeping a bend to his back or maintaining the sloping of his shoulders that he found went a long way so long as he could keep his mind in the part.

He clipped his now-empty skin to the belt he wore and gazed across the open market that had sprung up across from the expanse of the Jaw'l processing factory.

Baraq Waganat.

Jee was almost certain that the quadar hiding in the *hedgie* job line was the traitor. He'd squeezed three street whelps before he had plucked the lead that had brought him here, but it seemed to have panned out.

Watching the job line for only a single hand had made him as certain as he needed to be that the information was correct. One of those quadars did not move, but instead sat steadily, gazing out over the territory before him.

Jee spent money on the *aska* and watched for an extra hand's-worth to be sure, though.

Now, as he heard the gathering grow agitated, and then saw the quadar stand and rush away, he was beyond certain.

He would recognize the movement anywhere. The gentle limp. The slight lowering of one shoulder. Jee had spent many heats working on that body once. He didn't need to hear the name of Lelo filtering on the distant wind to know that quadar's identification.

Leave it to Baraq Waganat to do something as sentimental and as suicidal as to take on his dead son's mask.

Jee's eyes danced as he watched Tierra's brother leave the site. His chest beat with the excitement of the hunt.

He considered following directly, but that would risk letting Baraq know he'd been marked.

Jee El knew where Baraq would be now, and even if he lost the trail, the words Lelo ringing in his ears meant he'd be able to connect again.

The city was filled with primaries.

It was only a matter of time.

CHAPTER 30

Baraq pressed himself into the rising shaft of a broken cave.

The twisted passage had been narrow to begin with, but now pressed in so tightly he worried he might have to retreat to avoid trapping himself in the darkness.

The presence of the Amat'tesh facility loomed just above, though.

He could feel it.

After hours creeping through the chaotic network of wild caves, he was close enough now that the somewhat sweet aroma of its machinery filtered down to him, an odor comprised of equal parts exhaust from the chamber's engines and residue from the products those engines created.

He was so close. So close.

The Amat'tesh specialized in creating liquid fuels, and this mining operation—located underground and far from the Family's general compound—was at the core of their business. Like the Jaw'l operation he'd been looking at earlier, it also fed the operations of several other Families.

Stop the fuel, stop all those engines.

Kerosene-based liquids came from further processing of these sources.

He wanted the place dead.

He climbed farther.

The sound of the works thrummed in the enclosed space.

The low rumble of the engines came through that same rock that pressed against him so tightly, its vibrations playing over his fingertips, which were splayed and sensitive.

He imagined operations above him: Workers feeding those engines the rich ore that others had mined from below, engines and ovens converting it to various grades of energy sources that still more workers and more machines would pump away through a series of aqueducts.

At first, Baraq had planned to destroy those transports rather than the factory itself, but he chose this direction for the same reason he'd chosen to make his spidery way through the wild caves rather than take the more direct route of stealing into the mine shafts themselves.

The transports and mine shafts were guarded.

The wild caves and engines were not.

Surprise should give him the advantage he needed.

The schedule was on his side, too.

Rumors said the top members of all the Families would be in council now, bickering, arguing, and putting false faces on decisions that the Families had each already decided on.

The Tegra, with their stranglehold on weaponry, were prime movers. But the Amat'tesh powered the city, and the Banit Family fed it. These three would be in the position to wield control as things grew tight, with the Tegra and Amat'tesh being the real brokers. The rest would jostle and work to align with these three.

The best case meant two of them would emerge.

Worst case would see everything in control of only a single Family—with power delegated among others who would pay fealty to the one.

Baraq's bet was on the Tegra—which was why he still fixated on the poor results of his first foray into the Tegra storehouse.

The Amat'tesh were an elite Family, too, though.

To cripple them would be to cripple all Esgarat City powers at once.

With luck, this time things would go better.

Turning his head to fit, he pressed himself farther into the narrow gap. Proximity to success refreshed his sense of purpose. He moved calmly and surely, as the mountain required, his central reading even the smallest heat variance in the stone around him so that he could leverage the shaft's hollows and ridges to their optimum advantage.

Those heat patterns were the difference between life and death now. The passages were twisty and dangerous, but in so many ways they always felt like home. They reminded him of when he was a whelp and he'd play in dark caves under the Waganat compound. He'd first undertaken the practice simply because he enjoyed the sensation it gave him—being alone with the rock, moving carefully through it, feeling his ancestors and the age of his species as it had risen from the depths those many generations before him.

The tight, wild passages under the land taught him most of what he thought was important.

That play had given him the skills he'd needed to escape his brother the first time. Now he was using those skills to do the one thing he most needed to do.

Damage the Families.

Make his son proud of him.

Help the *hedgies*.

The aroma of the facility's processing lines above him grew thicker as he squeezed through the gap. The rumbling of the engines grew full-throated as he pulled himself through a final stage and found the thin crack that he recalled from his youthful adventures.

It opened on a diagonal, leading into a dark fold in the rock—a distance from the machines.

Before emerging from the passages, he pulled a polished mirror from small pouch he'd carried with him, and edged it around the corner, positioning it to see the zone where carts of ore rolled in.

His memory had been correct.

The chamber was expansive, its walls carrying the marks of excavation over generations. The Amat'tesh had cut two ventilation shafts into the ceiling, one for exhaust to escape and the other to let in fresh air. A pair of grinders stood nearby, aligned side by side, their twin flywheel shafts spinning in blurs.

The grinders took in chunks of raw ore and broke them into smaller, more transportable pieces. These smaller pieces were then transported to follow-on stations where ovens would cook them down into the base slurries the Amat'tesh needed to refine into fuels.

Across the chamber were a series of openings, pathways that led deeper in the mining areas.

A heavy *tal* beast emerged from one, huffing under the strain.

Three dark, dust-covered quadars followed, driving the beast, which pulled a rolling cart full of ore toward the grinder farthest from Baraq.

Bracing himself, he examined the path to the flywheels more closely.

They were the key.

Break them, or simply block them with something strong enough to defeat the machine's torque, and the engines would destroy themselves. They rotated in a blur behind the engines, their radius coming to less than a hand's gap away from the chamber's floor.

Get a big enough piece of rock wedged into the right place, and the machines would strip themselves.

That was the plan, anyway.

Execution was another thing.

His gaze took in chips and shards of detritus scattered around the grinders. None of those chunks looked big enough, but there was a piece of good fortune nearby. A battered plank of fiber board—a piece from a damaged cart—lay in a pile of refuse discarded close to the nearest engine.

It gave him some ideas.

Timing had to be right. If he wanted to disable both engines, he was going to need two pieces large enough to withstand the flywheel's momentum. Nothing in the area would serve—except for chunks of ore that the quadars were dumping into the loading bins. They were large enough but acquiring them meant he was going to have to pick his timing carefully—find moments where carts of ore would capture the attention of the workers.

That meant prolonged periods of waiting.

If he found the right moments, though, he could grab one large rock at a time.

The gap between the mountainside and the engines was tight, too, and made even more dangerous by the open flywheels rotating like scythes.

The engines were beastly things—snorting their loud rhythms

in the enclosed space and releasing enough heat that at least they would cloak Baraq's presence once he was behind them. They were easily big enough he could use them as shields.

He drew a breath and felt his muscles stretch. It had been a long descent and then climb to get here, and Baraq was no longer a whelpling. His body, though trim and strong for his age, was no longer flexible. It did not heal well.

If he got himself caught up in the gearing, he might as well hope those wheels simply ate him up.

That was it, though, he thought as he concocted his final plan— gather two large pieces of preprocessed ore, then center the fiberboard on a smaller rock to act as the fulcrum leverage point. If he placed one larger rock on the fulcrum itself, he could lever it into a roll targeted at the gap between the rotating wheel and the stone floor. As that rock traveled its path, he could dash off to push another by hand.

It would be dangerous.

He was going to need to work quickly and surely, which meant finding a way to ignore the fear of being so close to the flywheel.

It could work, though.

If he created enough havoc, he had a reasonable chance of using the ruckus as cover to race back to the crevasse and disappear.

Maybe.

CHAPTER 31

When it came to dirty work, Jee El held one truth to be above all others: All *hedgies* had their prices, and most of them were lower than one would think. When he lost track of Baraq, it hadn't been hard to find one willing to shovel information on this new "Lelo."

Jee supposed he should have followed orders and just killed the old quadar when he first caught his trail again. That's all Tierra had asked of him, and that would have been enough.

But he could learn something if he followed Baraq for a while instead, and with Tierra in a difficult position his liege would appreciate a little sweet to go with the root. So, he followed Baraq.

Followed as Baraq had picked his way out of the city and into the outer fields, then up a trail and into the mountain.

Where was he going?

It was an interesting question. A mystery. Jee pondered it each step of the way, working hard to the point of using only Baraq Waganat's latent heat points for his own steps to ensure Baraq wouldn't note him.

Following had been a wise choice.

Would he find the rest of the Ring?

Could he take out the entire gang at once?

He wanted to see Tierra's expression when Jee revealed whatever truth he might find.

The expression on Master Waganat's face alone would be worth more than the accolades such an achievement would bring him.

Jee followed at a distance into the early heat hours as Baraq slinked his way through the foothills and into the lowest regions where the rock became ponderous and massive, to where the sharp edges of the striated cliff face broke into plates that gave handholds and toeholds. He watched as Baraq disrobed to his basics, then used those toeholds and handholds to scale the rock, slowly and certainly, and eventually disappeared into a small gap high on that cliff face.

Jee El waited then.

He untethered the gray hood of his uniform and pulled its fabric up over his ears to protect himself as Eldoro rose toward his greater peak.

After he was certain Baraq was not planning to emerge anytime soon, Jee El slipped from his place of hiding and went to the depression in the craggy cliff wall where he had seen Baraq place his possessions—as meager as they were.

There he found the handgun.

He stashed the weapon quickly into his belt, along with the handful of Tegra bullets that were in a bag tethered to a looping belt.

He glanced up the cliff face. Considered whether he should follow Baraq before deciding otherwise.

Better to wait, he thought.

Time was now on his side.

CHAPTER 32

The *tal* arrived near the loading bin of the farthest engine.

Quadars got to work unloading huge chunks of ore into the bay. The engine whined with earsplitting screams as it took the new load.

Baraq made use of the diversion to slink to a space behind the engine closest to himself.

Calming his hearts, he reached to grab the fiberboard.

Yes, it was good fortune.

The board was a piece of a broken cart—as tall as Baraq, and still sturdy.

It would serve as he'd envisioned.

The engine radiated heat that was almost scalding, and which made the wait unbearable. He found a time, though, and slipped between the two engines far enough to pick out a somewhat rounded piece of rock big enough to work but barely small enough he could carry it the short distance back to his position.

He dropped it but screaming engines drowned out the clatter that might have otherwise exposed him.

A rest later, he had duplicated the acquisition.

Patiently—one slow movement at a time, each made between workers' trips to the engines—Baraq rolled the two stones to their positions. Waiting for the final break in attentions, Baraq let his imagination flow to the Council of Clans. Had it started yet? Had the councilor called the membership to order?

It would be a heated exchange.

Likely already having built to a peak tension before the session started, then threatening to bust open at every phrase.

He felt that tension here in this room.

Waiting.

Knowing—or at least hoping—that there would be at least two such explosions here in a moment.

The opportunity arrived.

Baraq set the equipment, one rock at the end of a seesawlike lever, the other a short push from its target, then triggered the lever hard enough to send the first rock rolling to the flywheel.

He ran to the other before seeing the first rock hit its mark.

He heard it though.

The flywheel crashed against rock with a dying wail louder than a cascading mountain landslide. The engine ripped the chamber with a force that nearly caused him to stumble, stripping itself, parts grinding, clawing, screaming, then popping.

Baraq pushed the second rock forward, feeling the deadly weight of whirring cast iron flywheel so close he thought at first it might have severed his ear. His reaction was instinctive. With a final push, he crammed the second rock forward, then leapt away, crashing himself so hard against the mountainside rock that he thought he'd lost his breathing.

The impact of flywheel on this rock sent shards flying.

The sounds of two engines killing themselves pierced Baraq's insides.

He ran, though. Scampered per his plan, back to the tiny, shadow-darkened crack that barely existed in the back of the Amat'tesh chamber.

He slipped in.

Then downward.

And downward still into the mountain passages that had birthed his species. Into the crevasses where one day—perhaps—he *would* actually become trapped, into the mountain passages where the answers to life's most difficult questions were most likely to be found.

He did not know it then, but when Baraq Waganat finished his climb, when he was gone from the Amat'tesh chamber, leaving two smoldering engines broken in the chamber, the world around him stood changed.

CHAPTER 33

Jee El woke from a deep sleep to find a form kneeling above him, pinning his body, a knife blade pressing in at his throat. The face of Baraq Waganat filled his view.

Jee started but controlled himself well enough to stay alive.

It got worse, though.

Baraq, wearing his ratty wraparound and *kami*, had the point of a second knife—certainly Jee's own—pressing into the soft gap between his back plate and his side. He wasn't certain the Waganat had it in him to do the deed, but one hard thrust and the knife would slice into his primary heart. If that happened, Jee would bleed out in an extended but certain death.

He had to have been deep in sleep to let his adversary come so fully upon him.

The Waganat's stench alone should have woken him.

Baraq waited with an essence of infinite patience.

Once certain Jee was awake and in control of himself, Baraq spoke in a voice dry with bitterness.

"I thought too long about killing you when I had the gun, Jee El," he said. "I'll not make the same mistake with these knives."

Jee slowly turned his open palms toward Baraq. "Do you always talk so much when you should be busy killing?"

The skin around Baraq's eyes flushed anger.

"What do you want?" Jee said.

Jee had taken this position because it was in a nook protected from the heats and because it was in higher territory than the crevasse Baraq had just come from. He hadn't meant to nap, but the place was so pleasant—cooler for being upslope and subject to thermal breezes. He'd watched the world move around him for a long time. The *pax* and the *piela* and *rela*. Flyers, too, soaring. It had been peaceful, and Jee was admittedly tired.

He'd been lulled into complacency.

Made a mistake.

"I want my weapon," Baraq said. "And while you are at it, I want you to carry a message for my brother."

"And that message would be?"

"He cannot hide."

"And why would he want to do that?"

"Because I'm going to kill him. I'm going to be like an insect to him, always stinging. And when he lets his guard down even once, I will take his life just as he's taken mine."

"Then that will be the last thing you do," Jee replied.

"So be it," Baraq said.

The pressure increased. Jee thought he felt blood well.

His senses were growing sharper now that he was coming to full senses. The pressure of the knife against his skin told him Tierra's brother was serious, but still the idea felt farcical. Baraq Waganat may have a knife in his hand now, but he was no match for Jee. If he could keep Baraq talking, he could complete his duty after all.

"And the weapon?" Baraq said.

"It is under me," Jee replied, a tingle of fear rising.

Disbelief showed in Baraq's hazel-touched eyes. His central dilated before he seemed to conclude Jee was telling the truth. He raised the knife that had been against Jee's shoulder gap to cross it over the other at his neck. There was no mistaking the line of blood that ran down Jee's neck to pool at his collar this time.

"You've changed," Jee said, knowing now that he had to be careful if he wanted to come out of this alive.

"Reach it out," Baraq said. "Slowly. Two fingers. Barrel first. If I see anything else, the mountain will take you back without anyone knowing it."

Jee gave an almost imperceptible nod, then slowly slid the gun out.

"Shove it away from you."

The gun skidded with a solid sound.

Keeping blades on Jee's neckline, Baraq rose.

Jee remained motionless while Baraq retrieved the weapon, stood firm, and checked the chambers to find them still loaded. Once convinced, he pointed the weapon at Jee.

"I thought you wanted me to carry that message to your brother?"

"I do," Baraq said. "Otherwise, you would already be dead."

He raised the barrel and backed away, first one slow step, then the other, showing his teeth in an expression that carried both anger and desperation. He looked tired to Jee, but tired in a dangerous way.

A moment later, Jee was alone on the side of the mountain.

Yes, he thought, putting his hand to his neck.

Baraq Waganat had changed.

COUNCIL

CHAPTER 34

This time, unlike others when Tierra Waganat had disdainfully decided to attend a session of the council, the chamber was full.

The Festia Family was here.

The Kat'all. Denari, Tael, Otara.

And, of course, the Tegra matriarch.

Members of every Family and clan in existence—even the agricultural Banit Family, despite their reclusive nature—had come to this discussion, their voices now combining to make a single mind-numbing barrage of sound that Tierra simply could not follow even if he tried.

Councilor Pelorit walked among them all, greeting each in that self-smug fashion he'd created from cycles upon cycles of such displays, pressing hands together at each stop, chatting with that quiet animation that tried so hard to suggest everyone here were all just the closest of friends.

Tierra hated it.

He was a creature of movement and action rather than one of words, but his distaste for the council went deeper than simply his gut-ripping dislike for the public posturing of social politics. He did not like the location—resenting even the time it took to arrive at the place. He did not like the formality of it all, the stilted airs of tradition that smothered him as soon as he so much as stepped into the place, even among the quadars who did nothing but maintain it.

The whole thing was nothing more than a different version of the intellectual halls of philosophers or the sanctimonious dens of preachers and priests.

Even the building itself, the massive, echoing hall carved so ponderously of basaltic stone from the mountains—each third segment provided by one of the three primary clans—spoke of overbearing pretension. He did not like the carved fiber root that had been treated, then cut into hard composites and formed into the seats each council member sat upon. Did not like the rings of Family boxes that stood, each in their proper ranks, and arranged to focus on the podium from which Councilor Pelorit—who as far as Tierra could say, remained councilor at his advanced age for the express reason that no one else was foolish enough to want the position—meted out his procedural malarky.

Council work, Tierra thought, as he prepared to watch the spectacle that was likely to play out before him, had never been his strength. That was among the reasons he'd recommended his brother for the role of council ambassador back in the days when their father had been looking to punish Baraq.

Pushing this onto Baraq dealt with two problems in one step.

This time, however, because he had asked Pelorit to call this session for the express purposes of airing Tierra's own grievances, he could not avoid such attendance.

So now Tierra sat on his hard seat—wearing the traditional robes that he most hated—in his Family's box at the back ring of the ancient chamber, staring impatiently up the polished walls and to the open gap in the ceiling where the light of Eldoro cast an already encroaching shadow down the pristinely rounded wall.

The temperature was rising.

The aroma of baked dust grew prevalent, and the weight of Tierra's robes grew more oppressive.

That he was alone didn't aid his discomfort.

He would have had Jee accompany him, but his advisor was away now, hunting Baraq under Tierra's own orders. His absence was for the better, but it also made Tierra aware of just how much calmer he was when his main advisor and compatriot was beside him.

He fidgeted with his walking stick and drew an exasperated breath just as Councilor Pelorit worked his way up the raised dais to begin the affair.

"All right," Pelorit said, balancing himself by clutching the edge of the polished stone podium. "I think it is time we began these proceedings."

Still several Family members continued to chatter until Pelorit hammered the traditional triangular stone against the podium to officially call the gathering to session.

"Thank you," he said as the membership each found their places. "As most of us already know, I have called this session of the Council of Clans as result of a Family claim."

"And that Family is?" a voice called.

"The Waganat!" answered Ceri Tah, the council representative from the Amat'tesh Family.

A rolling grumble of voices rose, and Tierra felt pressure from gazes.

"Fellows!" Councilor Pelorit gave a fierce call to chastise the attendees, clapping the stone again to generate a relative silence. "We will follow proper rules of decorum while in this chamber."

"The Waganats started this whole mess," Ceri Tah said.

She was young for a council ambassador, but Tierra knew looks and pedigree could be deceiving. Ceri Tah was sharp-minded, if not still impetuous. She had also been one of the few council members inclined to listen to the far-fetched blathering of Lelo, but had not, as far as Tierra knew, fallen in fully with his thinking.

Right now, the young Amat'tesh was staring darts at him.

"They are the ones that created this tension by leading the attack on our own population," she said.

"We all participated," Tierra replied.

Arguments broke out.

"Enough!" the councilor exclaimed again.

"All right, Councilor," Ceri Tah said after the rowdy gang settled. She had calmed rapidly, which made Tierra more unsettled than before. "What is the claim?"

"The Waganats have provided the council with reports that members of several Families have removed property from the Waganat stores."

"That's ridiculous," Ceri Tah replied just as a new wave of dissent broke out.

"They are not requesting compensation," Councilor Pelorit said over the crowd, "but instead are asking this council to confirm or deny that such actions are limited to only the Waganats."

As the request settled, an interesting expression crossed Ceri Tah Amat'tesh's face—a mix of interest and respect that added to Tierra's assessment earlier. The young quadar was quickly growing into a true force. He wondered if he might be able to speak with her afterward, and—if so—whether the conversations might be beneficial.

If Tierra was going to get out of Azat Tegra's clutches, he needed to do something that would give him leverage over the Tegra Family. An alliance with the Amat'tesh would serve the trick.

"Let me get this fully into my mind," Olan Festia said. "Tierra Waganat is insinuating that we are each stealing from his Family, and at the same time is asking the council if we are stealing from each other as well?"

"I will not stand for this kind of talk," said Asha Denari, whose Family was from clan Hlrat. She wore her most regal of Hlrat robes, the folds of which she had draped primly in the proper spots as she sat in her box. Even in the heat, she glistened with a perfect application of the *witze* oils her clan considered proper public wear. Tierra could make out its aroma from across the chamber.

The representative's uncharacteristic outburst said everything about the emotions around the room. The elder Denari had been a member of this guiding body for many terms and had been part of several important actions taken by the council. For her to be as aggressive as this was unsettling.

Asha continued.

"The Denari Family has never stolen from another Family—especially not one in such desperate need as the Waganats are in today!"

"Ah, the essential Denari!" called out M'ran Kat'all, who was from Tierra's own clan Terilamat and also an elder of the council.

"And what is that to mean?"

"The Denari have always been fluid in their positions."

"This is a lie!" Asha replied. "We are always steadfast in our commitments."

M'ran gave a harrumph.

"That is quite hard to believe coming from a family who had so many defections."

Voices erupted.

Asha stood at that insult, pointing a gnarled finger at M'ran, with whom she shared a long history of such conflict. The chamber had heard M'ran's story of defections—about a pair of Denari youth who had run to the mountains to join Louratna's community—often enough that the story had become threadbare.

Still, it worked.

"You and all of your Terilamat clans will refrain from using our name in that fashion ever again," Asha called out.

"I wouldn't be surprised to learn it was Denari hands that have been behind the rash of renegade vandalism plaguing us all," M'ran added.

"You will refrain from such attacks now!" Asha said.

"Or what?" M'ran said. "You'll bury me in a pile of mudbrick?"

"Fellows!" Councilor Pelorit called again. "No one is accusing any Family of these vigilante attacks!"

The Denari seethed, but finally kept her head as another round of raucous arguments echoed through the chamber.

Tierra stifled a laugh, and locked eyes with Azat Tegra.

Of all the quadars in the chamber, she seemed most stoic, which gave him less satisfaction than he thought it should. They had an arrangement. Or at least he thought they did. Now a ball formed in his lower stomach that he wasn't sure he liked.

The sensation of neutrality that adorned the set of Azat Tegra's central wasn't as strong of a feeling as he'd hoped for.

He grew worried.

Despite the enjoyment that came with watching the Families argue, Tierra wondered if he might have misread the situation. He remained sure Jee El's reports were true—that the Families *were* each preparing for the worst while pretending to keep the peace between them—but he was growing concerned that it was far beyond the point of no return. He had planted this seed in Councilor Pelorit in hopes of forestalling outright war among the

Families, and Pelorit had run with it. Now the Families were all too prepared to eat their own.

Had he gone too far?

Clutching the rounded head of his father's walking stick with such intensity it might crack, Tierra stood, pounding it solidly enough against the polished granite floors that he finally captured Councilor Pelorit's attention.

The councilor, looking for anything by which he could regain control, clomped the attention rock loudly and pressed the gathering for quiet.

When that quiet finally came, his voice cracked with concern.

"I think it's time to let the Waganat Family speak for itself," Pelorit said. "Tierra Waganat, you have the floor."

Tierra cleared his throat.

Gazes turned his way.

"My fellows," Tierra said. "I, above all of us, understand exactly what has happened to the status of the Waganat name. I will not lie to anyone here and suggest that without the most generous support of Azat Tegra and the use of her Family's defensive mechanisms, we would not even be here. For that, the entire Waganat Family thanks you, Azat. As we thank all the Tegras before you. Our Families' relationships have been strong since the times of our elders' elders."

He bowed toward the Tegra box, feeling Azat's distant bemusement as more question than acceptance. She wanted to know where he was going. His choice to make their arrangement so public was a calculated gamble, but a gamble nonetheless.

"You cannot hide behind a gun, Tierra Waganat!"

It was Olan again, elder ambassador to the council of the Festia Family.

"I know you would like to see us fall, Olan," Tierra called out quickly. "As do many of you. Let's not fool ourselves about that, either. I hear the accusations, for example, about the role my brother might be taking in these otherwise random attacks on the Families, and I know you would want Baraq to be responsible—as if he would return to this city and take on his son's mantle. And I hear your anger at the Waganats taking the lead on the actions that squashed Lclo to begin with—as if you've suddenly forgotten that you were *all* in agreement with the action itself, and that you *all* had a part to play."

Voices rumbled, and Tierra raised a hand as a shield, then gestured at Olan once again. For the first time since the beginning of the session, the silence was both natural and absolute.

"I see that benefit for you, though. My father was an outstanding business partner, but not well liked—perhaps with good reason. I'm not here to debate these past histories, but it is a fair argument to say aloud that there are many who would enjoy putting the Waganat grounds on focus while we are weakest.

"I want you each to know, however, that we do not want this conflict. We are all dealing with the repercussions of our collective action against Lelo. That is so obvious as to not need stating. We Waganats are obviously in a troubling time, but that will not always be the case. So, I warn you: Do not misread the Waganats' state for true weakness. Like a wounded *neantha*, no good can come from challenging us now.

"Think of that next time you direct an action against one of our shops, and as you think of that I recommend you also consider this request as warning that you should keep your centrals peeled for actions of all who sit around you. You know who you are. You are not the only Family attempting to grow fat as you remain in wait to see how the winds will blow next for us."

"Where is your proof, Tierra Waganat?" It was Ceri Tah. "You come to the session citing Family claim, and yet you have nothing beyond a list of names that any *hedgie* with half a cycle of teachings could have scratched."

Other members rumbled.

"Ceri Tah is correct," Olan said from his Family box. "We cannot trust the Waganats. We all know that, do we not? Ranya Waganat was a quadar who changed courses whenever the sand became more advantageous in the opposite direction. His *sons* are no less trustworthy."

"That is what we are all saying in our cloistered councils, is it not?" M'ran added. "With the unmasking of Lelo as a member of the Waganat Family, and the knowledge that it was the Waganats themselves who slaughtered both their own whelp and hundreds of others—actions that have brought us all to this brink of anarchy—we cannot afford to allow them to repair themselves."

Tierra crashed his walking stick to the floor.

"With Tegra guns at our hand you cannot afford to—"

"We all have Tegra guns, you fool."

Voices echoed in the chamber.

Tierra glanced quickly to Azat Tegra but received again only a neutral reaction in return.

The truth hit him, then.

She was playing the field.

He had hoped their alignment was stronger than it had been, had hoped that a certain degree of exclusivity would attract her to the idea that Waganat communications combined with Tegra weaponry would be enough to control All of Esgarat together. But the Tegra were in position to save whomever they approved of— or at least to be on the good side of as many Families as they could support with weaponry.

He could already hear her arguments: *It is no business of mine when any Family uses our weapons to defend themselves.*

It all added up to say Azat Tegra had grander plans than sharing control of the council with another Family, leastwise not the Waganats. Instead, she was nudging herself closer to control of the entire body.

He gazed hard at Olan Festia, then.

The same Olan Festia who was a direct ancestor to Crissandr, his brother's pair-mate.

The Festia Family had been bitter with Crissandr's decision to leave them for a Waganat, a Family that, while at least Terilamat, had always treated them as somehow lesser.

Which was only proper.

The Festia Family had never been among the truly well-respected of the Terilamat. Olan had hoped that the addition of a Festia to the Waganat Family might change that ranking, but to Ranya Waganat's eyes the inclusion served more to reduce Baraq rather than raise the Festia.

"The Festia will never have Waganat property, Olan," Tierra said, a sense of anger rising. "You may all well have guns. But I can promise that if nothing else, I will use the Tegra guns *we* have to ensure that Festia hands never touch a Waganat property again."

A deep silence came over the collective.

The intensity of stares grew hotter than Eldoro cresting high.

From behind Tierra came the grating of the huge doors that led out of the meeting chamber as they swung open against the stone floor. Bathed in Eldoro's blazing light, a bustling message runner entered.

"We are not to be interrupted while in session," Councilor Pelorit said gruffly. "What is it?"

The messenger strode down the central pathway to the podium at which the councilor stood, then turned into the Amat'tesh box, handing a crisply folded page to Ceri Tah, the young representative of the Amat'tesh Family.

In the dead silence of the moment, Ceri Tah hesitated, then read it.

"Is this true?" she asked the runner.

"Word came only a moment ago."

Ceri Tah turned to Tierra, the paper notice still dangling in one hand.

"Our factory has been destroyed," she said, turning to face Tierra with newfound rage in her expression. "Reports say that the culprit was your brother."

It took another beat for ramifications of this to fall upon them.

When it did, chaos filled the chamber.

MOUNTAINS

CHAPTER 35

Pella was trying not to be unhappy. It wasn't her fault that Anko Banit had followed her back to Nectani Gap. Ezi had scolded her and sent a dispatch to escort the Banit whelp back to his Family. Feeling unfairly chastised, she had retreated to this most secret of her hiding places.

From behind a bramble patch that acted as cover for a small shack, Pella quieted her breathing. She hunched down and peered between branches to where the small hole in the side of the wall seemed to taunt her.

It was getting late in the heat—only little Katon remained in the sky, low on the horizon, but her young eyes could still make out the hole. It was a *pax* den, long abandoned but still good for practice.

She'd found the hidden shack a cycle before, made of some thick vine, and broken brick, and desiccated wood that had mostly rotted in the burning rain, all mortared with mud that had cured in glumpy patches. Whoever built it had made sure it was tucked behind a ridge of stone, high enough up the mountain to give a view of the city if she climbed up the ledge.

Its roof was slanted downslope and provided patchy shade through much of the heat.

Holes in its walls funneled mountain drafts to provide cooling.

The place was as abandoned as the *pax* hole, probably built by a *hedgie* family who had been trying to live close enough to the city but outside the control of the Family Council.

Sometimes when she came here to be alone, she would make up stories about the quadars who once lived here. They were always good quadars. Always with several whelplings. Always running from the Families. Sometimes the parents would play games with the whelps or make up stories.

Now, though, she wasn't pretending.

Now, as she took in the target her hearts stilled and a sense of mindfulness settled over her. She pictured the stone she held in the fingertips of her throwing hand, imagined it whistling across the open space to crash into the hole.

It would be a tough shot, but she had been practicing every day for most of the cycle.

Dangerous times called for such diligence.

That's what Ezi said so often, and what she had repeated to the gathering a few hands earlier, before the elder Sister Vareta spoke up and forced Ezi to kick Pella out of the circle again, and before Anko made his sudden appearance.

"This is no talk for a whelpling," Vareta had said, motioning toward Pella who had perched herself in her usual corner of the gathering room. Pella fought the urge to mock her.

Though Pella knew Ezi didn't agree with Vareta on this, and though she knew Ezi would tell her everything that happened, Pella felt an anger toward Ezi that burned hotter each time she thought of it. Ezi should have stood up for her. But instead, she had still sent Pella away and then blamed her for the young Banit's arrival.

She furrowed her brow at the memory. The bitter taste of anger came up from her stomachs to coat her tongue.

She did not like Vareta. Did not like her at all.

Pella may still be a whelpling, but she was growing quickly. She had earned the right to be there—and she was already versed enough in the way the world worked to understand that having Ezi recall conversations was no substitute for the real thing.

The rock's edge was sharp against her fingers.

Regardless of what grown quadars like Vareta thought of her, Pella wasn't going to lose another family. This time she was going to be prepared.

Deliberately, Pella moved the fabric of her shift so it wouldn't impede her throw.

In a swift motion, she stepped out from behind the brambles, reared back, and let loose the stone. It whirled through the air as it looped toward and then—with a satisfying clatter—crashed into the hole. She quickly transferred a second stone from her other hand, and threw again, this time missing the mark by only a small sliver.

"Hmmm," she said to nothing but the mountainside. "Not bad for a whelpling."

She bent to pick up another rock.

Hurling that one, too, she scored another direct hit.

As she was bending for another stone, she heard a crack from westward, further up the slope.

She froze.

She had been coming to the mountains for some time and had grown accustomed to the creatures of the area. This sounded more like quadar than creature.

A heavy step. *More than one.*

Pella cautiously ducked into the brambles again.

At least two intruders were higher up on the mountain, heading her direction. She edged farther back, and a flash of fear burned in her chest.

She reached both hands to gather stones.

This is my place, she thought. *I'll fight off any* hedgie *who tries to say otherwise.*

Worse ideas spilled into her mind then.

What if these weren't *hedgies*?

What if they were Family agents? What if they were spies?

Enemies who followed her after the gathering had expelled her.

If true, what else did these spies know?

What had they seen or heard?

Had she put Ezi and her other members of the Ring in danger?

A spike of anxiety chilled her veins as all these thoughts flashed through her head.

A voice gave a huff from behind a ridge that opened to the shack. Another voice came, too, an odd voice to Pella's ears. It made a stream of something that sounded like words but were not.

A moment later the two quadars came into vision.

Only it was not two quadars.

It was one—a female.

And another creature, built like the quadar but taller and without a central. Its skin was raw and red. Thin white fur covered its head.

The two were struggling, leaning on each other—or better noted—the quadar leaned on the other creature with each of her awkward steps, and the other somehow managed to stay afoot. They moved that way, as if a single creature, a lurching step at a time, each one bringing grunts and moans and strings of "words" from the creature.

Familiarity struck her then.

She had seen the female.

Maybe?

Is this the pair-mate of my Baraq?

Pair-mate of the quadar she'd met in the dungeons of the Waganat facility.

With a hurried step, she emerged from the brambles.

"Crissandr?' she said.

CHAPTER 36

Torrance's vision blurred.

The pain that was his entire existence flared step by step, again and again. Muscles giving, catching, shaking. The skin of his face, hands, and arms searing with every twitch. His throat was dry and clenched tight. His tongue bloated and raw. Every breath drew stifling air across cracked skin.

He was in a classroom, trying to answer a question that had no answer.

Marisa? He thought he might have called out.

He raised his hand and saw Louratna at the head of the room, but when she called on him the words that came from his mouth were gibberish.

He felt Crissandr fall against him.

Heard her incoherent groan from somewhere a galaxy away.

Wrapped his arm tighter around her waist, though even that movement brought stabs of pain lacing through his hands. His body was on fire. His skin cracked and blazing red. His eyes dry and so rough against his lids that it burned to blink. Breathing brought air to sear his throat.

He smelled fire.

Tasted dust tinged in blood.

He was dying.

He knew he couldn't let go of Crissandr—that to let go would be the same as to stop breathing. Crissandr was the only real thing in his life now. The only thing that mattered. He clutched her for everything he was worth, feeling the tether of her arm around him as if it was salvation.

His head pounded.

The clatter of Crissandr's walking stick clapping rock set his mind to a jazz recording he'd once heard. Then he was lying in bed, white static washing over him as an invisible cloud in the darkness. *Take a chance*, a voice came through the haze. *Take a chance, right?* A memory then. He was in a memory. Was it earlier this heat—or a week of heats ago? Huge birds with massive wingspans, soaring in the sky above, screeching among themselves like vultures waiting for their meal to simply fall over and die.

His tongue was thick as sandpaper on the roof of his mouth.

The road seemed to stretch out behind them.

Days, he thought.

They had walked for days, and even the two-go hadn't been enough to keep them sane without water.

Had they walked through Eldoro high?

Crap. Crap. "Shouldn'ta done that," he said.

Crissandr might have moaned in reply.

"Shouldn'ta done that," he said again.

Or was that a lizard's grunt?

Water, he thought. He would kill anything for just a sip.

They fell into each other again, Crissandr and Torrance, their shared rhythm the only thing that kept them both moving. The need to put one step before the other simply to avoid letting the other down.

He clutched her robes in both hands to stay upright.

She grabbed at his.

"This is what it's like to die?" Torrance asked.

Crissandr simply clutched at him again, moving beside him.

He grabbed her harder again.

Holding on.

Pushing his leg ahead of him as she did the same on her side of the tandem.

"Yes," he said. "This is what it's like to die." He laughed, unable to crane his neck up to look for buzzards. "Could be worse."

There was a house.

A house?

Too small for a house. A cottage on a lake. He remembered that. Peanut butter sandwiches with sand in them. He was twelve. Ready to swim. Ready to jump into the lake of … *water*. A house. A boathouse. Skiing. A dive again into … *water*.

"I don't want dinner," he said when his mother called him in. The lake beckoned him. *Water*.

Water.

He jumped into it. Let the dark liquid crash over his head before realizing he couldn't swim.

"Bullshit," he said. "I know how to goddamned swim."

Crissandr tumbled.

She was just weight now. Pressing him down farther into the black currents.

Then a girl stepped from behind a bush, and he was embarrassed to find himself naked.

"Crissandr?" the girl said.

WAR

CHAPTER 37

The sounds of conflict rang over Esgarat City.

Voices screaming. Parents calling for their whelps, lovers calling for their mates. The clatter of Tegra guns. The flashing of Pew'tal knives. The city smelled of fear and desperation. Quadar blood spilled in crimson pools that turned green in the mud before clotting into globular rivulets.

There could be, the Families knew now, only one victor, and to that victor would go all the spoils that remained behind.

As a result, the city burned.

In the distance, all around the ring of mountains that many quadars considered as containing All of Esgarat, the land burned, too—though not with fire.

No plumes of smoke or crackling of flame.

No screams of the living within.

In these silent lands filled only with the sounds of jah calls and neantha howls and foliage rusting in the breeze, the burning came more slowly, a dry baking rather than a searing flame.

Yet, burn the land did.

And, in the high above, Eldoro fell again, following the path that its physics required it to follow. Meanwhile, a spacecraft made a jump from one place in the universe to another, siphoning fuel from Eldoro, known to the ship captain as Alpha Centauri A.

Its radiation drained, the power of its helium and hydrogen fusion dynamics faded, burning down deeper through its core.

A different flame.
A different burn.
On that spacecraft, a clock ticked second after second. Marking time as it slipped by.

CHAPTER 38

Tierra returned to what had once been the boundary of the Waganat compound to find its fate laid out in the clearest of terms.

His hands shook as he took in the land.

His primaries burned with a sense of loss as deep as he could ever recall.

Fires burned from several places across the expanse—which had once seemed so immense. Debris from sheds and barracks and garden grounds lay broken and scattered over the rolling land. Now smoke billowed over the grounds. Now the workers had fled—some leaving tools to lay on the ground, work only half done, at best. Walls still unbuilt. Barrels and troughs of mudbrick left standing unpoured to cure in the baking rays of Eldoro falling.

And the dead were here, too.

Already the dead.

Castaada, his body beaten into a bloody mash, was more identifiable by his uniform than his features. Another armed cousin had been shot—likely with his own weapon, which was nowhere to be found.

Tierra could not tell if the revolt had been quick or not, but it had been successful.

All Waganat security posts had been abandoned, and already independent quadars and other Families were picking over the place.

It's over, he thought.

Esgarat City was in chaos.

The Waganat line had no defense.

It was, Tierra understood with acidic certainty, most certainly over.

He should leave, he thought. Leave now. He didn't want to know what would happen if he were captured. It depended, he supposed, on the Family that did the capturing.

He turned.

The familiar form of Jee El emerged from a street ahead, his form shrouded in smoke and dust. Tierra's advisor strode toward him, his gait still strong despite the loss of everything.

The big quadar's presence calmed Tierra, again.

He pulled at his ceremonial robe, tugging it into proper place as he waited for his advisor to come to his side.

"Where have you been?" he asked when Jee drew near.

The big quadar's gaze took in the entirety of what had been the Waganat compound before landing on Castaada's body.

He drew his hand up, fingertips distractedly running over the soft place at his neck.

Tierra noted the knife line.

"Tracking your brother," Jee said. "As you requested."

"Baraq," Tierra said.

"Yes."

This is all Baraq's doing, he thought. All of it.

The thought gave him a spark of happiness.

For an instant, Tierra had fallen into the mistake of blaming himself for this. For that same instant he had felt embarrassed and weak. He had taken over a robust Family from his father. Now look what he had done with it.

That thinking was wrong, though.

He remembered that as soon as Jee had spoken.

His brother.

It was Baraq Waganat, not him, who had destroyed the Family's underlying defenses. Baraq who had whelped Brada—who had become Lelo and who had subsequently required such a public extermination. Now it was Baraq who had set a spark to this kindling by destroying the Amat'tesh production facility.

"You have found him."

"Of a sort," Jee said. "He has a message for you. He says he's going to kill you."

Tierra both laughed and clicked.

"I believe him to be the renegade vigilante everyone is chattering on about."

"Is that so," Tierra replied in a caustic tone. "If only we had known that sooner."

Jee's expression betrayed that Tierra's response hurt him.

"Can you find him again?" Tierra said.

"Shouldn't be hard. The *hedgies* and others have taken a liking to him."

"Stupid *hedgies*."

Jee said nothing. Just scanned the terrain. Behind them came a boom in the distance. "We should leave," he said. "Katon will fall soon. We need to find shelter before darktime."

Tierra felt smug inside.

Loyal to the end, he thought.

He clicked agreement and hefted his walking stick, waving it as a sword. "Then let's go."

"Will we rebuild?" Jee asked as he strode beside Tierra.

"Someday," he said. "Maybe."

Though he knew even then that he could never pull it off.

His father could have, but Tierra was not his father.

He didn't see a way he could do it now.

Later? After the struggles faded and the city was in disarray? Maybe. His strength was not in public politics, but he knew other ways to get things done.

"I am with you either way," Jee said.

"I know you are," Tierra said. "And I will always remember that."

They set out to the north, toward the slopes his Terilamat ancestors had come from.

"What will we do now?"

"Find Baraq, and give him what he wants," Tierra replied.

Jee's grunt suggested uncertainty.

"I will give him a chance to kill me," Tierra said.

CHAPTER 39

As Baraq suspected, the Tegra Family was ready this time.

It was a heat after the war started, but that wouldn't have mattered. They were on guard even before the city began ripping itself apart—before gunfire rang out, before the puttering motor carts and skippers roared to life to take desperate quadars either racing to claim land for the Families or, though there was nowhere to go but the mountains, trying to get out of the city before the harshest of fighting began.

His imagination had gone wild before, but it was harder watching this happen in real terms than he had ever imagined it could be.

Still, here he was, lying on his belly, on the roof of a six-story tenement building a distance away—which he had chosen since it was both close enough to get an unobstructed view and because it was the tallest in the area that wasn't the Tegra warehouse. The near-complete exodus of its *hedgie* occupants made for less complicated scaling of its floors, too.

Azat Tegra had already doubled her security after his first foray into their stores.

Now she'd doubled it again, all while adding the extra fire power of their most advanced weaponry to the guards she'd deployed. Weapons she'd heretofore kept secret from the public.

Now was the proper time to disable her, though.

To wait longer would be to enable Tegra domination, and Tegra domination would be worse long term.

He had selected the Amat'tesh as his biggest action yet in hopes the loss of their machinery would raise tensions, and thanks to the fortuitous timing of the emergency council session, it had worked like a charm. The fulcrum that had maintained the city's balance was breaking, and if Baraq could draw Azat's attention from the fray—if he could damage her now—it would throw the entire city into even greater turmoil.

This next action would be vastly more dangerous than his others—more dangerous than even that of his push through the cave systems under and around the Amat'tesh factory, not the least because his cave work had left him already deeply fatigued. His fingers, toes, shoulders, and knees all throbbed with pain that came from the use of new muscle, and those new muscles stiffened as he sat still in preparation of the next step.

Eldoro's heat was harsh on his back plates.

The building's broken roof creaked and crumbled as he edged slowly to a position where he could see what he needed to see.

Those sounds from the roof did nothing to ease his fears.

Having come up through the building's tangled mishmash of stairwells, ropes, and handmade ladder rungs, Baraq considered it a miracle that the building itself was still standing.

The gun he carried in his belt—looped under the robe he wore to blend into the rooftop—was hard against his hip, which also still ached from his earlier escapades.

Reaching the edge of the building, he raised a hand to shield his gaze.

The Tegras had built this warehouse in the farthest southern reaches of the city proper because it was away from prying eyes yet still had an easy approach. There was, as far as he knew, no hidden door here.

Unlike the weapons store at the city's center, the Tegra storehouse was more a fortress than a building. Its external walls were eight stories tall and built into a hexagon that was mostly open to the sky. Each of the six walls were thick, buttressed brick, with each intersecting point having a small platform at its top.

Each of the platforms housed placements of huge, bowlike weapons that pointed downward, each already loaded with a large, iron-tipped javelin, and each operated by a pair of quadars—one, he assumed, would load the device, the other would point and fire.

The guards on the ground carried long rifles slung over shoulders.

Portals opened in random patterns up and down the walls.

Back in the ages ago when he was a member of the Council of Clans, he had been in this storehouse three times, so he understood well that those portals served the dual purposes of providing defensive positions as well as giving ventilation to those inside the storerooms.

He also remembered that inside were a collection of stacked compartments that lined the walls, each filled with stockpiles of guns and ammunitions.

On the ground, two buttressed doorways gave the main point of egress. He would find another at a wall toward the back.

He counted eighteen freestanding guards, two stationed at each doorway and the rest equally scattered across the warehouse yard. Catapult launchers built at the center of each of the hexagonal building's walls would give longer range support. The Tegra had dug pits around the perimeter, long lines of burning ditches the guards could light from any one of five stations he could see.

This was not going to be easy.

He smiled at that.

Even while he was a member of the council, Baraq had seen Azat Tegra was both dangerous and reliable to her word. She was not among the quadarti leaders Baraq had considered to be sloppy or underprepared in their approaches. He liked the fact that she managed her debts and her assets with the precision of a perfectly drawn design.

She was, he thought, like Louratna but without Louratna's compassion and with Louratna's love of discovery replaced with a passion for winning.

Now his stomachs churned.

He would circle around.

Strike from the southern desert just before the lesser Katon faded to join her greater brother—the time when heat profiles wavered between the cool of night air and radiating heat from the ground. That meant he had two hands of time to get out of this dilapidated building, and then wind his way through the city outskirts and out to the desert to approach the fortress from the wasteland.

That was the most opportune direction for a lone quadar like him. If he managed his body temperature properly, he could use the horizon's lensing to approach safely enough.

If he was lucky, anyway.

Full armies would not attack from that direction, so Baraq was betting that security focus would be a bit less oppressive on that backside.

He didn't like to think about what would happen otherwise.

Regardless, the true challenge would be finding a portal built low enough that he could scale quickly and avoid attention.

Finished with his recognizance, Baraq edged himself backward, away from the ledge, listening to the tired building creak and moan as he moved.

After a distance, he rolled to stand.

He turned to the ladder rungs that led downward, stretching his muscles to try to wring out the ache. He was tired, but he had to get going if he was going to make it into the desert in time.

Which was what he was thinking when he found Tierra Waganat standing beside the ladder hole—Tierra, his brother, primaries blazing orange in the fading light of Eldoro, standing awkwardly at the opening to the ladders, with Jee, his hired muscle standing calmly beside him.

Tierra whipped his heavy walking stick around before pounding it against the palm of his open hand.

"Good heat, brother," Tierra said. "I received your message."

CHAPTER 40

"You are still dressed for the council, I see," Baraq replied, mostly to take a moment to let this turn settle in his mind. His brother's garb was council formal, but now torn and ratty.

"No, Baraq. I am dressed for your sentencing."

Tierra stepped forward.

The cane whipped in the air as he twirled it.

Baraq reached into the slot in his robe, fingers suddenly clumsy as he grabbed for the gun.

The cane struck his wrists with a sickening crunch, and Baraq gave a wail as he fell to his knees. Rubble tore through his robe to shred his kneecaps. The wrist roared with a ball of fire, first, then pulsed with lightning.

"I should have had you killed a long time ago," Tierra said, beating Baraq over the shoulder with an impact that felt like a brand.

Baraq caught himself before he fell flat, though.

There was that much.

Tierra reared back for a blow aimed at his head.

Baraq pushed his throbbing hand through his robe and down to his belt, grabbing the gun and firing randomly as he raised it.

The retort echoed over the city.

The roofing shuddered as Tierra fell to it, clutching his thigh and screaming in quadarti curses as a cloud of white and gray dust rose in the late heat. The sound of a timber cracked below him.

Then another.

"You shot me!" the Waganat gasped, blood flowing crimson brown between his fingers to drop to the rooftop.

Baraq was breathing heavily now.

His plan for the Tegra warehouse was dashed.

Even if he survived, the sound of the gunshot would send the Tegra guards into heightened states of anticipation.

Instead, he was face-to-face with Tierra, his brother who had killed his son, the head of his own Family who had destroyed everything Baraq cared about.

Beggars cannot be choosers.

He drew himself to a steady position and leveled the gun.

"I told Jee what I was going to do," he said, aiming at Tierra's central.

Jee's boot came as if from an invisible space in midair. It took Baraq in the ribcage and ripped breath from him with as much certainty as if he had reached down Baraq's throat and clawed out all three of his hearts.

He fell hard to the roof.

There was no air. No breath. Only the stagnant, cloying aroma of dust, dirt, and heat. Only the echoey sounds of something Baraq thought might be distorted laughter. Only the taste of dirt. Dry and claylike. Then the pain from that kick arrived, and Baraq thought he might never want to breathe again. *Ribs*, he thought. Pulverized.

The gun he'd held had clattered away, laying now on the very precipice of falling off the roof.

Jee's next kick fell against Baraq's thigh.

"Don't kill him, Jee," Tierra's voice came through the mire of his senses.

Baraq's brother was standing again. Leg glistening with blood, but standing, leaning on the stick as he wobbled over to him.

"He's mine."

Baraq wondered if Tierra would beat him senseless with their father's walking staff, or whether he would grab Baraq's gun and make it quick.

The former, he decided. Tierra had a score to settle, and the price would be as dear as he could make it.

The stick stuck Baraq across the back.

Pain filled his entire body.

The stick reared back again, when from behind Tierra came a loud crack and the *whumpf* of air leaving lungs.

Both Tierra and Baraq swiveled their gazes in time to see Jee's body crumble to the rooftop.

A loud screech of ripping timber came from the building below Jee. The floor gave a single hard lurch downward, and then came another crack.

That was when Baraq saw Oast'el standing where Jee El had fallen. Oast'el, his son's childhood friend and Orange Ring collaborator. The young quadar stood, bare chested, but wearing an Orange Army weapon sash looped over his shoulder. His striated arms flashed in the last rays of Eldoro. A thick club angled from his hand.

Crawling up from the ladder hole behind him was Ezi.

Her face was just rising over the ledge when another loud crack echoed from below.

Oast'el made a move toward Tierra.

Another loud crack came from the floor below Jee and below Baraq.

Shards of fiberboard plaster and wiring crumbled.

His legs flew upward, and suddenly he was in free fall.

A piece of flooring flew past from above him.

He landed hard on his back, stunned again when the back of his head hit the hard floor below. His vision blurred and a shell of pain flowed from his skull.

Jee's body dropped beside him, too, falling to the floor to become a rumpled and motionless form.

Tierra, too, had fallen, but he had better fortune.

Primaries wide, Tierra used his cane to lift himself up. His glance went to Baraq, then Jee El, but rather than finish his attack, he hurled himself, limping, but able, at a rope that dangled in the ladder hole. He caught the rope and swung there for a moment, whining with pain, then after he stabilized, he dropped the cane and quickly lowered himself.

"Nwahhhhelpt," Baraq said, unsure why or what he was saying.

He tried to raise up but couldn't bring himself to do so.

He blinked to try to focus.

Then—was it only a moment or a cycle of moments—Ezi's face appeared over him. Oast'el's next.

"Can you carry him?" Ezi said.
"We'll find out."
Then everything went black.

FALLOUT

CHAPTER 41

Ezi came to the nook they had laid the Torranze in.

It was sleeping, its breathing a rhythmic pattern interrupted with series of moans, whines, and grunts. Its cracked skin had glowed crimson and oozed yellow oils. She wasn't sure but it seemed she could see the beginnings of the black rot beginning on a spot high on one cheekbone. It had been sleeping since Pella had reported its arrival and they had brought the creature along with Crissandr to their caves.

Pella had been attending them both, dribbling thin streams of water into them, ensuring blankets and pillows were always in place.

Scanning first from the Torranze's huddled body to the chisel-marked walls of the cave, Ezi wondered what its arrival meant. She ran a pair of her long fingers over a line of scars in the rock, wondering about the quadars who first hollowed this alcove.

What did they use the room for?

To store grain perhaps?

To house a whelpling?

She pondered the timing of the Torranze's arrival, coming now as the great city burned in the gap below and the end of everything else seemed so near. At one point it had called out Louratna's name—which confirmed rumors that the two had been close.

She knew what it was—this Torranze.

Ezi had first heard of the thing from Brada, who had learned of it from Baraq.

The Torranze and the Light That Fell from the Sky.

There was some connection there.

Baraq had brought the Light to Louratna in the first place. Then later had come the Torranze, and it too had gone to Louratna's mountains.

That had been a long time ago, or at least it seemed that way to her. Time moved in strange ways, though. Truth said it had been only a few cycles, just as truth said it hadn't yet been twenty hands of heats since her Brada had been taken from her.

As she watched it sleep, Ezi felt an overwhelming sense of inadequacy.

She didn't understand.

Why it was here? What was it doing?

She couldn't help but feel like the Torranze's arrival played a part in her life, but she couldn't fathom what that might be. Watching it sleep made her feel useless and weak.

Footsteps came from behind.

Pella, followed closely by Oast'el.

The whelp went to the Torranze's side and poured water from a larger clay decanter into a smaller cup. The creature coughed and sputtered as she dribbled it into his mouth, but in the end he drank.

"*Mata,*" Pella said, running her hand across its brow.

Ezi looked at Oast'el.

"Baraq is alert again," he said.

CHAPTER 42

Baraq Waganat stood at the edge of a cliff face that gave a view of what had, until now, been the greatness of Esgarat City. The back of his head throbbed, and he was certain he had broken some ribs. The rest of his body ached, too, and he felt the kind of fatigue that seemed to grow from the center of his bones.

He had to see this, though.

Had to take in the city with his own primaries.

So, he stood carefully here, tenuously holding himself upright, and he breathed the air, and he felt the presence of the mountains around him as the city burned below.

The cave system Ezi and the Orange Ring had brought him to was in the northern slopes, which reached so majestically up into the domed sky above him. As a Terilamat, these were his home slopes—the range of the mountains that had, if legends were true, birthed his entire line of quadarti. To the east and west rose the homelands of the Kandar and Hlrat clans.

It was this ring of mountains that gave the quadars the homeland that was now crumbling before his eyes. He thought of them. The Families. Each branching repeatedly over the cycles, each claiming their own areas of expertise, each gnawing out their own living from the harshness of the lands around them.

How different were they each?

He remembered a late darktime a long time ago when he had taken the Taranth Stone—The Light That Fell from the Sky—to

Louratna, and she had explained how the mountains cut the heat and gathered what rains would come. How those rains gave the land to support quadars. Louratna's voice returned to him then, low and steady as if it rode in the dark cloud of smoke that grew over the city.

She had said this time would come.

It was the mountains that gave the Esgarat this life, she said, but it was also the mountains that constrained it. Those constraints, she argued with Baraq, create envy, and jealousy, and greed.

It was the Families that will cause the problems.

He should have believed her when she predicted such things, but he had not.

He was a Waganat, then.

He still believed in himself.

His gaze went to the farthest area south—out into the harsh, open, dusty lands of the free desert.

All of Esgarat, he thought, then snorted.

Footsteps rustled behind him.

"Ezi," he said without turning.

"Who else would it be?"

Baraq winced. Little Pella had told him of her discovery of Torranze and Crissandr, so they both knew the answer to that question.

Ezi came to his side.

"The city will be no more," Baraq said, his gaze scanning the landscape.

"Not as we knew it, anyway," Ezi replied.

He gave three noncommittal clicks and glanced to the double heats of Eldoro and Katon. Eterdane was in the sky, too, sitting on the eastern horizon now—its tiny light too weak to cut the sky. For some reason he thought again of Hara, his first whelp, the daughter who had been taken from them too soon. He recalled holding her high, lifting her up as far as he could reach as he listened to her clicky giggle.

"I don't think it will matter," he said. He clicked again, absently. "If Torranze lives, maybe he can tell."

They stood like that for some time. Silently. Watching smoke roil from the city to swirl in a circular flow of hot current. Ezi's presence was firm and solid. She had been his son's pair-mate, and now he felt the air stirring around her as she breathed.

The wind blew in their silence, though.

Baraq smelled the scent of the parched *banka* trees upwind.

"You understand we are not taking no for an answer this time, *Dada*," Ezi said, using the honorific that came from her tie with Brada.

"I understand."

"You will lead us, then?"

He felt a knot in his gut at the question. "You are the Orange Ring's leader," he said. "Don't pretend to me you don't know otherwise."

She stared at him with judgment in her gaze.

"I said I understand. I will fill a role as the rest of the free quadars expect."

"All right," Ezi said. "But I understand you, too."

"There's not much to understand."

"If we're going to be honest about what we know and what we do not, then I need you to stop that."

Baraq focused on her.

She was right. That was his true problem.

"I have spent much of my life pretending about who I am," he said. "I may not know how to change."

"It is never too late to start," Ezi replied, then put a hand on his elbow. "That was something Brada would say to quadars as he would leave their homes. I can help you."

He stared at her, his hearts feeling a leap of hope.

"Brada chose wisely," he said.

"Maybe he did," she clicked. "But if so, then wise choices of *kalla* passes through the generations."

He cleared his throat, feeling an undercurrent to her comment. Understanding its intent. He clenched his fists, then relaxed them. Stared out over the distance one more time. Then, drew a breath and let it out slowly.

"Is Crissandr well?" he finally said.

"She is injured," Ezi said. "But with rest she will recover. I am not as certain about the Torranze."

Baraq gave a gruff wheeze as his laugh. "Torranze," he corrected. "His name is simply Torranze."

She clicked.

Her primaries blazed and the curl of her lips grew warm.

"If he lives, I'll know better."

Baraq nodded, then with a final glance out to the burning city, turned to Ezi. "Where is she?" he said.

"Come," she replied. "Let me show you."

CHAPTER 43

Crissandr was awake when Baraq entered her compartment. It was a small cut in the caves, far enough back that foot traffic was only dim in the distance. Her shape was familiar in the dim light of luminous moss. The draw of her breathing was also familiar.

He basked in the familiarity of her heat.

She was silent at his approach.

She sat cross-legged on a deeply worn rug of wide, woven fiber, and leaned against a padded pillow that she had propped against a wall. Her *haldi* was torn and ragged, unchanged from her travels. She had eaten, a fact revealed by the collection of hard *havra* shells piled beside her.

He could see her fatigue in the empty droop of her shoulders and the deep lines in her face as she craned her gaze his way.

It was, he saw, a fatigue that went beyond the physical.

She had completely drained herself, and now she appeared tired in that threadbare way that quadars got after having seen and borne too much.

"Crissandr," he said, stepping closer.

"Baraq."

The tone to her voice was hollow.

"May I sit?"

She motioned the floor beside her. Cautiously, fighting his own pain and feeling his own suffering, he took his place a distance apart, his back pressing against the cool cave rock.

For an instant he felt good, simply sitting with Crissandr, breathing the same air. He fought an urge to grab hold of her hand, knowing that would be … wrong. Instead, knowing it was his place to start, he put the back of his head against the cool rock, and gathered his words.

"I still see that day," he said.

Haltingly.

He took a breath. "I cannot help it. Every time. When I close my primaries. I still see Brada's body, bleeding on the dais."

"I know. I see it too."

"I don't know what to do with that."

She clicked softly. "Nothing," she said. "That's what you do with it."

He sighed.

"Some things are not meant to pass," Crissandr said. "I think that is good, though. I do not want to forget."

Baraq put his head in his hands, unable to say what he was thinking for many long moments.

"Thank you for that," he finally replied. "It is how I feel, too, though I did not have the courage to say it. I cannot let Brada go."

"You have always had enough courage, Baraq."

"No. If I did things would be different."

"You did what you needed to do."

"I left you."

Crissandr drew a familiar breath but remained silent.

"You needed me, and I left you. That is the opposite of courage."

Crissandr gave a low, negative click.

"There was a time when I would have agreed with you, Baraq. You chose to return to the city rather than stay with me, and that hurt. I was angry. I can't lie about that. But then I saw what the Families did in the mountains."

"And?"

She clicked, then sipped from a water cup to dampen her lips.

"Then I understood. They would not stop. You saw what was happening before I did, and you tried to stop it."

"I didn't see anything," Baraq said.

"You felt it, though. You did what you had to do."

Baraq saw a presence in Crissandr's gaze. A strength that wasn't there a moment ago. She had always been so practical.

Always so direct. Her expression now carried both of those emotions.

She spoke again.

"I'm sorry I made you choose between Brada and me when you left the mountain. I was in pain, too, and I turned away. But—whatever your reasons, you did a right thing. Brada would be proud of you."

"Thank you."

The words stuck in his throat.

Crissandr lifted the water bowl to him, and he took it. The drink went down hard, but it went down.

He placed the bowl back, then gathered himself.

He locked gazes with his *kalla*, his pair-mate, and in that moment every cycle of his life flashed before him. He took in Crissandr sitting before him, and saw nothing but the youthful quadar he had met at a community celebration so many cycles before. Saw her dancing. Blue cloth of a billowing *haldi* flowing in her wake, firelight dazzling in her primaries.

He felt her body beside him.

Felt the warmth of a life lived together.

Finally, he took a breath and asked the only question that mattered.

"Have I destroyed us?" he said.

Crissandr shook her head. "No," she said. "I am proud of you, too, Baraq."

She lifted her hand, then, and Baraq took it, twining his fingers into her grasp.

"I am your pair-mate," she said.

"And I am yours," he replied.

CHAPTER 44

When he woke, Torrance Black found himself in a coarsely cut, rounded cave room, curled into a tight ball and unable to move. His body burned with heat so hot he thought he was going to combust. His stomach knotted together, the skin of his body stretched so thin and so tight he couldn't move without pain knifing through his body.

The only time he tried to roll to his other side, he nearly passed out.

There was Pella, though. Little Pella—the dreamlike quadar he and Crissandr had stumbled upon and who, at first, Torrance through was simply a hallucination—who came to his side and gave him first water and then thin slices of *dashtar* fruit that helped untangle his belly.

The water soothed him.

The sharp fruit burned against his cracked lips, but eventually gave him strength.

It took three heats before Torrance could reason again, during which his skin had cracked and peeled, then cracked again.

It was another heat before he could sit and then walk.

Crissandr spoke to him that first day, explaining.

Pella had found them.

Esgarat City was in ruins—or at least in the process of becoming ruins before whichever Family "won" the war might someday begin to put it back again.

Torrance shook his head as she explained.

"There will be no rebuilding," he said.

He knew better. He had felt the changes during their trip that before he had simply surmised.

Given the technology here, the kind of work required to build back could take generations, and in the most relative terms it would be only a few scant years before this planet would be unable to support life—or at least not the life that was here now.

Esgarat—this planet that humans called Eden—was doomed.

"The Families don't understand what's going on."

"That is nothing new," Crissandr agreed. "Though Baraq understood that well before I did."

Torrance laughed, then looked at Crissandr.

"Baraq?" he said, cautiously. "He lives?"

"Yes," she replied. "He is here."

"That is good," he said, thinking.

The news was bleak. Without a city, or with a city under some form of oligarchic authoritarian Family leader, he couldn't get his mind around how he could help. All he could say for sure was that it sounded like throwing rockets into the mix was certainly a Very Bad Idea.

Still.

He thought about Baraq. He felt a connection, a sense that he'd been in communication with this quadar since well before they had ever met. Baraq, he knew, was the faceless being he had in mind all those distant years ago when he had reprogramed the wormhole pod that the quadarti now called the Taranth Stone.

"I want to talk to him," he said.

Crissandr clicked affirmative. "*Adiago nar,*" she replied. Tomorrow. She indicated the blankets he had been sleeping on. "*Adia nar,* rest."

He got the idea.

Despite his protestations, he was asleep a few minutes after she left.

CHAPTER 45

When Torrance next woke, he found Crissandr had left him a gift of the walking stick she had used on their ill-fated trip. It gave him a moment of joy. Standing hurt, but he could do it.

The walking stick helped.

He took a tentative step, pressing hard on the stick.

A rustling came from the open gap to his chamber. "I thought I heard you stirring," Crissandr said, leaning against the rocky opening.

"Yes, I'm up," he said. He lifted the stick. "Thanks for this."

"Welcome?" she replied, using the English word.

"Yes, welcome," he said. "I'll try to not scare any *tal* beasts with my speed."

She clicked affirmative. "That would be wise."

A few moments later, they emerged from the caves.

He blinked against bright skies, taking time to let his eyes adjust.

Alpha Centauri A was near the horizon now, Katon close behind. That meant the time of year was growing closer to what the quadarti called Convergence—the period when Katon the lesser had nearly caught up to Eldoro as the greater heat raced to fall below the horizon.

"Where is Baraq?" he said.

She guided him to the cliff where Baraq and Pella sat together. The older quadar was telling the younger a story. Something about a little whelpling named Hara who rode in the stars. Torrance hadn't heard that legend before, but it was coming to an end.

He'd ask about it later.

He made a seat out of a rocky outcropping and waited.

The view was spectacular. Unlike the never-ending expanse of heat-cracked desert that sprawled from Louratna's northern side of the mountain, the entire panorama here consisted of a ponderous horseshoe ring of mountain peaks that roped in the horizon to the east and the west and reached up to the sky behind them in the north. The towers of Esgarat City lay in the basin below—tiny, really, relative to the behemoth cities in human existence, but massive for All of Esgarat. Far to the south, the dust-filled desert loomed in the distance. The land where quadars lived, though, while not fully green, was darker and richer.

It was, he thought, an amazing testimony to life that this basin could do so much with so little.

When Baraq came to the end of his story, he sent Pella away and came to join him.

"You wanted to speak?" Baraq said in a halting mixture of the qualish Torrance had built with other quadars.

Torrance glanced at him quizzically.

"Crissandr is teaching me words."

"I see."

"Many to learn."

Torrance gave an involuntary chuckle, then used the cane to indicate the land before them.

"It looks different from this side."

Baraq gave an affirmative. "Louratna's cave gave out to the desert."

Not knowing exactly why but feeling a powerful need to connect with this quadar, Torrance held his right hand out.

Confused, Baraq took it in his.

The grip was firm and warm. Baraq's six fingers were longer than Torrance's five, and they wrapped around the back of his hand the entire way, engulfing him.

A sense of wonder hit Torrance so hard it nearly broke his heart.

He remembered how it felt to stand on the gunmetal platform on *Everguard*'s System Command and give the direction to launch wormhole pods, watching his data screen as it reported one of those pods had peeled off to fall toward the planet, and hoping the errant piece of technology could change the course of that planet's history.

Now he was sitting on a cliff of that planet with the creature who had been involved with that pod's analysis, and who might now be the only chance that planet's inhabitants had to survive.

Torrance cleared his throat. "Crissandr told you that I came to offer you rockets?" he said, trying to gear himself up to learn a new form of qualish.

Baraq gave a soft affirmative.

"Not want now," Baraq said. "Not *mata*."

The answer brought him relief. It was over. There was no way for the Orange Ring to "win" a war, and even if they did the result would be so bloody there would be no workforce of a size needed to make the rocket he'd planned to send into space.

His grand plan wouldn't work.

"No," he said. "They wouldn't help now."

Torrance felt the hard rock of the mountain below him. Felt the breeze. Felt the remnants of Baraq's grip on his palm and fingertips.

He had to tell Baraq exactly what was happening to his planet but found it hard to speak.

He was certain Louratna had introduced Baraq to the idea of what the wormhole pods had done to their home star, and it wouldn't surprise him if Baraq had put enough pieces together to come to the conclusion himself, but there was something horrifyingly wrong about telling someone you know their planet is dying so rapidly that whelplings like little Pella were unlikely to see a natural end.

"All of Esgarat *indati*," he said in a single blurt.

"*Indati*?"

"Yes."

Baraq gazed directly at Torrance now, but Torrance found he was unable to meet the gaze.

This was always how it was always going to end, though.

He realized that now.

Reverse engineering at this level of complexity was nearly impossible. And even once they put the answer together, the technologies here—while growing—were simply too rudimentary to build anything that resembled a real spacefaring program. In a perfect situation, his plan with Louratna to rebuild the clouds would have given the quadarti another few cycles of comfort, but even then, it was simply buying time until human-driven ships flew enough missions to leave Alpha Centauri A a dark husk.

The truth of this lay in the burned husk of land that sprawled out below.

He had always known it.

Somewhere, buried deep in his core, Torrance Black knew he had played his part in killing this planet.

He tried to look at Baraq but couldn't.

Instead, he just nodded.

"All of Esgarat?" Baraq said.

Torrance finally forced an answer. "Yes. All of Esgarat is dying."

The quadar gave a harsh chuff.

Torrance forcibly wrenched his gaze to Baraq and saw a set in Baraq's gaze that told him he'd been right. This quadar had already understood what was happening. Not fully. But he had pieced together a truth before, and now he understood without doubt that his world was dying.

Resignation crossed Baraq's face, but he clicked a sad and almost inaudible affirmative.

Torrance shielded his eyes from Eldoro.

Baraq held his hands out before him, the six fingers of each spread wide. "So," he said, still looking down the mountain. "What are we to do?"

Torrance didn't know whether to laugh or to cry, but after stifling one of those immediate reactions he looked at Baraq and saw the quadar was serious.

"What are we going to do?" Torrance echoed.

Baraq pointed down the slope to the distant buildings. "All of Esgarat still breathes."

It was true.

And where a moment ago Torrance had seen resignation in Baraq's primaries, now he saw determination.

"It is never too late to start," Baraq said, a tone of something Torrance read as strength coming to the quadar's voice.

The heat was sharp against Torrance's still recovering skin, and he knew the black spot on his cheek was not going to get better, but the altitude and the breeze made for a pleasant moment in which he could smell the openness of the planet. It made him mourn for what could have been.

But Baraq was right.

Torrance had given himself to Louratna's memory. He'd come this far.

Suddenly he remembered sitting in his living room with his father and his mother, watching a university football game as the clock ran down and with his father's school—the University of Wisconsin—holding the ball, far from the goal line and behind by only a few points.

His father screaming *you gotta throw that ball into the goddamned end zone!* as the team ran a different play.

The memory raised hackles on the back of his neck.

Don't quit, his father had lectured him afterward. The game's not over till it's over. Torrance smiled at the image that flashed in his mind then: Louratna, wagging her big-knuckled finger at him and screaming for him to throw the ball into the end zone.

He smiled because she didn't use the profanity.

He felt better. Maybe.

He wasn't stupid, and neither was Baraq. Things were dire, but the game wasn't over yet.

"It's time for a Hail Mary," he said to Baraq. "Or maybe I should say it's time for a whole bunch of Hail Marys."

Baraq scrunched his face into a question.

"Don't worry," Torrance said, ignoring the unspoken question.

His brain was running on overdrive.

He'd been focusing on the idea of sending one big rocket toward the Solar System for so long it took a moment to shift gears.

"Louratna said you make radios?"

"Radios?"

"Wave talkers," Torrance added, using the pure quadarti tongue. "Louratna said you made wave talkers."

Baraq clicked affirmative. "Long ago."

"Can you make another one?"

"If I have parts. Should be."

"It has to be small."

"How small?"

Torrance grimaced. "I don't know." He held his hands into a

five- or six-centimeter circle. "Maybe that?"

"Possible," Baraq answered.

"All right."

Over the next hour, Torrance laid out his plan.

Instead of one *big* rocket, many smaller ones.

Instead of targeting the Solar System alone, a scatter shot everywhere. Each carrying one of Baraq Waganat's radio beacons and a note of some sort. Hundreds of messages at once. The ultimate space spam, he said at one point. Or a thousand, all blaring into the void in hopes someone would pick them up. If the quadarti couldn't go to the Solar System, bring the Solar System to them.

Without intense resources, Edart and her team could never manage to build the behemoth it would take to get his original idea off the ground, but he'd bet everything he'd ever had that she could arrange a production facility to make the smaller systems they'd need for this approach with nothing more than she had.

It was still a Hail Mary, but it could work.

It was certain this planet was dying, but there was still breath, and while there was breath, there was hope.

It was all that he had left to give, but if Baraq could make a wave talker to fit, Torrance was going to make it happen even if it was the last thing he would ever do.

The clock was ticking.

Time to get the football in the air.

When he had laid out his plan, Baraq's primaries carried a new fire.

This time it was Baraq who proffered his hand.

This time it was Torrance who took it.

He gazed over the mountain ranges.

"Torranze?" Baraq's question broke his reverie.

"Yes."

"Why?"

Torrance was going to ask for clarification, but then he understood the question.

Why are you doing this?

He also realized something else in that gaze.

He took a deep lungful of the mountain air from All of Esgarat and felt then what it meant to be a human being. He remembered the feeling that had come over him as he watched quadars line up their dead bodies. He recalled the feeling of Louratna's thin shoulders under the film of her fabric wrapping. He looked into Baraq's eyes and saw the same determination he'd seen in Louratna's and in Marisa Harthing's and several other people he had met along the path of his life.

The answer *because Louratna wanted it* wasn't enough. Nor was it simply because he felt guilty.

He laughed then, feeling oddly free.

"We have a saying where I come from," Torrance finally said. "Sometimes people say that we are all made of stardust."

Baraq gave an expression Torrance interpreted as a frown.

"It means that we are all the same inside. The atoms in my body are no different from atoms in yours."

Another frown.

"Pieces," Torrance said, picking at his skin. "Small bits."

"Small bits," Baraq replied, clicking again.

"We are all different, but not in ways that matter. Bits in my body are the same as bits in yours."

Baraq drew a breath. "We are all made of mountain."

"I like that," Torrance said, feeling a strength bigger than the moment. "We are all made of mountain."

EPILOGUE

As Karshi Fael arrived at Harshish Point early in the afterdark, the *neantha* still padded along behind her. She had grown to appreciate the beast. She found she liked the company. They made a good team. Its presence kept other dangers at bay, and her hunting and scavenging could keep them both fed.

Things had changed, though.

Even in the dim light she could see differences in the outpost.

Gone were the rough grasses that had led to its open entranceway. Silent were winds usually touched by hints of music or voices of free rangers playing their bone games.

The rocky plates, once covered in tangles of *katja* root, were now barren—only those angled such to limit Eldoro's harsh rays still smelled of the living leaves and blooms of the plant.

She saw no guards in the stands where she had expected to see them.

Karshi Fael trudged up the pathway toward the rocky outcrop that served as its main entrance, finding nothing but a whining wind that echoed emptiness.

The central chamber's troughs were dry, though when she pumped a few times, she could get a trickle to flow.

The water was cool on her throat.

She pumped more for the animal and stepped aside to give it access.

Further exploration showed nothing different from the entry.

Empty compartments.

Abandoned halls.

A few bottles of fermented *katja*, stoppered and left behind.

She breathed heavily in her fatigue.

Her back ached and her legs felt like rubber.

They would sleep here tonight, but there was nothing here for her.

It would be a long trip back.

She didn't know if she could make it, but the truth here was obvious.

Harshish Point was gone.

"I am sorry to bring you here, *neantha*," she said to the animal. "But I know of nothing else."

This is the end of

STARDUST

STEALING THE SUN: BOOK 8

If you enjoyed this story, you might be interested in the rest of
the series:

STARFLIGHT

STARBURST

STARFALL

STARCLASH

STARBOUND

STARCRASH

STARGAMES

STARDUST

STARBORN

If you enjoyed this story, please consider stopping by your
favorite online booksellers' websites and leaving a review. Word
of mouth is the most powerful force in the universe when it
comes to the livelihood of your favorite authors.

ACKNOWLEDGMENTS

Even more so than usual, I want to thank my first readers John Bodin and Sharon Bass for their helpful comments—with special kudos this time to Sharon who really helped me see what shape a major portion of this book needed to take. Thank you so much.

I want to thank everyone who has helped me over the past year, too. Pandemics suck. Difficult life events during pandemics suck, too. If you're a creative sort and we've made contact over the past year or two, you can count yourself among the thanked.

I want to thank my daughter Brigid, for pushing me into the Novel Dare this grew out of. Get thee hence and buy her books. You'll not be sorry.

And, as always, I want to thank my beautiful and amazingly gifted wife, Lisa, for her general overall support as well as her copyediting. Also as always, I can guarantee that if there's a flaw in this manuscript, I put it there after it passed through her hands.

ABOUT THE AUTHOR

Ron Collins is an Amazon best-selling Science Fiction and Dark Fantasy author who writes across the spectrum of fiction genres.

His fantasy series *Saga of the God-Touched Mage* reached Amazon's bestselling dark fantasy list in several countries. His short story "The White Game" was nominated for the Short Mystery Fiction Society's Derringer Award.

He has contributed a couple hundred or so short stories to *Analog*, *Asimov's*, *Fiction River* Anthology Series, and several other professional magazines and anthologies.

He holds a degree in Mechanical Engineering, and has worked to develop avionics systems, electronics, and information technology before chucking it all to write full-time—which he now does from his home in the shadows of the Santa Catalina Mountains.

Ron's website is: www.typosphere.com
Follow Ron on Twitter: @roncollins13

Sign up for his newsletter to get free stuff!

http://www.typosphere.com/newsletter

9 781946 176387